TAKE YOU-

add a million years of Progress, and you
have the man of tomorrow. You have enormous
power over your universe and twice as many
labor-saving devices as there are labors.

> **The world's at your feet!**
> **You're having a Wonderful Time!**
> **Everything's just GREAT!**
>
> **Only sometimes you look**
> **at what you've made—**
> **and it scares you half to death.**

This is the stuff of PILGRIMAGE TO EARTH.
The man of the future has all sorts of
marvelous things to make life easy, but it takes
his old-fashioned brain every minute of the
day to keep them going. It's a tough world
for humans, very bewildering, sometimes
grotesque—

A REAL COMPLICATED LIFE

Books by Robert Sheckley

UNTOUCHED BY HUMAN HANDS
CITIZEN IN SPACE

pilgrimage to earth

by

Robert Sheckley

BANTAM BOOKS • NEW YORK

PILGRIMAGE TO EARTH

A BANTAM BOOK PUBLISHED OCTOBER 1957

CONTENTS

PILGRIMAGE
TO EARTH

Alfred Simon was born on Kazanga IV, a small agricultural planet near Arcturus, and there he drove a combine through the wheat fields, and in the long, hushed evenings listened to the recorded love songs of Earth.

Life was pleasant enough on Kazanga, and the girls were buxom, jolly, frank and acquiescent, good companions for a hike through the hills or a swim in the brook, staunch mates for life. But romantic—never! There was good fun to be had on Kazanga, in a cheerful open manner. But there was no more than fun.

Simon felt that something was missing in this bland existence. One day, he discovered what it was.

A vendor came to Kazanga in a battered spaceship loaded with books. He was gaunt, white-haired, and a little mad. A celebration was held for him, for novelty was appreciated on the outer worlds.

The vendor told them all the latest gossip; of the price war between Detroit II and III, and how fishing fared on Alana, and what the president's wife on Moracia wore, and how oddly the men of Doran V talked. And at last someone said, "Tell us of Earth."

"Ah!" said the vendor, raising his eyebrows. "You want to hear of the mother planet? Well, friends, there's no place like old Earth, no place at all. On Earth, friends, everything is possible, and nothing is denied."

"Nothing?" Simon asked.

"They've got a law against denial," the vendor explained, grinning. "No one has ever been known to break it. Earth is different, friends. You folks specialize in farming? Well, Earth specializes in impracticalities such as madness, beauty, war, intoxication, purity, horror, and the like, and people come from light-years away to sample these wares."

"And love?" a woman asked.

"Why girl," the vendor said gently, "Earth is the only place in the galaxy that still has love! Detroit II and III tried

1

it and found it too expensive, you know, and Alana decided it was unsettling, and there was no time to import it on Moracia or Doran V. But as I said, Earth specializes in the impractical, and makes it pay."

"Pay?" a bulky farmer asked.

"Of course! Earth is old, her minerals are gone and her fields are barren. Her colonies are independent now, and filled with sober folk such as yourselves, who want value for their goods. So what else can old Earth deal in, except the non-essentials that make life worth living?"

"Were you in love on Earth?" Simon asked.

"That I was," the vendor answered, with a certain grimness. "I was in love, and now I travel. Friends, these books . . ."

For an exorbitant price, Simon bought an ancient poetry book, and reading, dreamed of passion beneath the lunatic moon, of dawn glimmering whitely upon lovers' parched lips, of locked bodies on a dark sea-beach, desperate with love and deafened by the booming surf.

And only on Earth was this possible! For, as the vendor told, Earth's scattered children were too hard at work wrestling a living from alien soil. The wheat and corn grew on Kazanga, and the factories increased on Detroit II and III. The fisheries of Alana were the talk of the Southern star belt, and there were dangerous beasts on Moracia, and a whole wilderness to be won on Doran V. And this was well, and exactly as it should be.

But the new worlds were austere, carefully planned, sterile in their perfections. Something had been lost in the dead reaches of space, and only Earth knew love.

Therefore, Simon worked and saved and dreamed. And in his twenty-ninth year he sold his farm, packed all his clean shirts into a serviceable handbag, put on his best suit and a pair of stout walking shoes, and boarded the Kazanga-Metropole Flyer.

At last he came to Earth, where dreams must come true, for there is a law against their failure.

He passed quickly through Customs at Spaceport New York, and was shuttled underground to Times Square. There he emerged blinking into daylight, tightly clutching his handbag, for he had been warned about pickpockets, cutpurses, and other denizens of the city.

Breathless with wonder, he looked around.

The first thing that struck him was the endless array of

theatres, with attractions in two dimensions, three or four, depending upon your preference. And what attractions!

To the right of him a beetling marquee proclaimed: LUST ON VENUS! A DOCUMENTARY ACCOUNT OF SEX PRACTICES AMONG THE INHABITANTS OF THE GREEN HELL! SHOCKING! REVEALING!

He wanted to go in. But across the street was a war film. The billboard shouted, THE SUN BUSTERS! DEDICATED TO THE DARE-DEVILS OF THE SPACE MARINES! And further down was a picture called TARZAN BATTLES THE SATURNIAN GHOULS!

Tarzan, he recalled from his reading, was an ancient ethnic hero of Earth.

It was all wonderful, but there was so much more! He saw little open shops where one could buy food of all worlds, and especially such native Terran dishes as pizza, hotdogs, spaghetti and knishes. And there were stores which sold surplus clothing from the Terran spacefleets, and other stores which sold nothing but beverages.

Simon didn't know what to do first. Then he heard a staccato burst of gunfire behind him, and whirled.

It was only a shooting gallery, a long, narrow, brightly painted place with a waist-high counter. The manager, a swarthy fat man with a mole on his chin sat on a high stool and smiled at Simon.

"Try your luck?"

Simon walked over and saw that, instead of the usual targets, there were four scantily dressed women at the end of the gallery, seated upon bullet-scored chairs. They had tiny bulls-eyes painted on their foreheads and above each breast.

"But do you fire real bullets?" Simon asked.

"Of course!" the manager said. "There's a law against false advertising on Earth. Real bullets and real gals! Step up and knock one off!"

One of the women called out, "Come on, sport! Bet you miss me!"

Another screamed, "He couldn't hit the broad side of a spaceship!"

"Sure he can!" another shouted. "Come on, sport!"

Simon rubbed his forehead and tried not to act surprised. After all, this was Earth, where anything was allowed as long as it was commercially feasible.

He asked, "Are there galleries where you shoot men, too?"

"Of course," the manager said. "But you ain't no pervert, are you?"

"Certainly not!"

"You an outworlder?"

"Yes. How did you know?"

"The suit. Always tell by the suit." The fat man closed his eyes and chanted, "Step up, step up and kill a woman! Get rid of a load of repressions! Squeeze the trigger and feel the old anger ooze out of you! Better than a massage! Better than getting drunk! Step up, step up and kill a woman!"

Simon asked one of the girls, "Do you stay dead when they kill you?"

"Don't be stupid," the girl said.

"But the shock——"

She shrugged her shoulders. "I could do worse."

Simon was about to ask how she could do worse, when the manager leaned over the counter, speaking confidentially.

"Look, buddy. Look what I got here."

Simon glanced over the counter and saw a compact sub-machine gun.

"For a ridiculously low price," the manager said, "I'll let you use the tommy. You can spray the whole place, shoot down the fixtures, rip up the walls. This drives a .45 slug, buddy, and it kicks like a mule. You really know you're firing when you fire the tommy."

"I am not interested," Simon said sternly.

"I've got a grenade or two," the manager said. "Fragmentation, of course. You could really——"

"No!"

"For a price," the manager said, "you can shoot me, too, if that's how your tastes run, although I wouldn't have guessed it. What do you say?"

"No! Never! This is horrible!"

The manager looked at him blankly. "Not in the mood now? OK. I'm open twenty-four hours a day. See you later, sport."

"Never!" Simon said, walking away.

"Be expecting you, lover!" one of the women called after him.

Simon went to a refreshment stand and ordered a small glass of cola-cola. He found that his hands were shaking. With an effort he steadied them, and sipped his drink. He reminded himself that he must not judge Earth by his own standards. If people on Earth enjoyed killing people, and the victims didn't mind being killed, why should anyone object?

Or should they?

He was pondering this when a voice at his elbow said, "Hey, bub."

Simon turned and saw a wizened, furtive-faced little man in an oversize raincoat standing beside him.

"Out-of-towner?" the little man asked.

"I am," Simon said. "How did you know?"

"The shoes. I always look at the shoes. How do you like our little planet?"

"It's—confusing," Simon said carefully. "I mean I didn't expect—well——"

"Of course," the little man said. "You're an idealist. One look at your honest face tells me that, my friend. You've come to Earth for a definite purpose. Am I right?"

Simon nodded. The little man said, "I know your purpose, my friend. You're looking for a war that will make the world safe for something, and you've come to the right place. We have six major wars running at all times, and there's never any waiting for an important position in any of them."

"Sorry, but——"

"Right at this moment," the little man said impressively, "the downtrodden workers of Peru are engaged in a desperate struggle against a corrupt and decadent monarchy. One more man could swing the contest! You, my friend, could be that man! You could guarantee the socialist victory!"

Observing the expression on Simon's face, the little man said quickly, "But there's a lot to be said for an enlightened aristocracy. The wise old king of Peru (a philosopher-king in the deepest Platonic sense of the word) sorely needs your help. His tiny corps of scientists, humanitarians, Swiss guards, knights of the realm and royal peasants is sorely pressed by the foreign-inspired socialist conspiracy. A single man, now——"

"I'm not interested," Simon said.

"In China, the Anarchists——"

"No."

"Perhaps you'd prefer the Communists in Wales? Or the Capitalists in Japan? Or if your affinities lie with a splinter group such as Feminists, Prohibitionists, Free Silverists, or the like, we could probably arrange——"

"I don't want a war," Simon said.

"Who could blame you?" the little man said, nodding rapidly. "War is hell. In that case, you've come to Earth for love."

"How did you know?" Simon asked.

The little man smiled modestly. "Love and war," he said,

"are Earth's two staple commodities. We've been turning them both out in bumper crops since the beginning of time."

"Is love very difficult to find," Simon asked.

"Walk uptown two blocks," the little man said briskly. "Can't miss it. Tell 'em Joe sent you."

"But that's impossible! You can't just walk out and——"

"What do you know about love?" Joe asked.

"Nothing."

"Well, we're experts on it."

"I know what the books say," Simon said. "Passion beneath the lunatic moon——"

"Sure, and bodies on a dark sea-beach desperate with love and deafened by the booming surf."

"You've read that book?"

"It's the standard advertising brochure. I must be going. Two blocks uptown. Can't miss it."

And with a pleasant nod, Joe moved into the crowd.

Simon finished his cola-cola and walked slowly up Broadway, his brow knotted in thought, but determined not to form any premature judgements.

When he reached 44th Street he saw a tremendous neon sign flashing brightly. It said, LOVE, INC.

Smaller neon letters read, *Open 24 Hours a Day!*

Beneath that it read, *Up One Flight.*

Simon frowned, for a terrible suspicion had just crossed his mind. Still, he climbed the stairs and entered a small, tastefully furnished reception room. From there he was sent down a long corridor to a numbered room.

Within the room was a handsome gray-haired man who rose from behind an impressive desk and shook his hand, saying, "Well! How are things on Kazanga?"

"How did you know I was from Kazanga?"

"That shirt. I always look at the shirt. I'm Mr. Tate, and I'm here to serve you to the best of my ability. You are——"

"Simon, Alfred Simon."

"Please be seated, Mr. Simon. Cigarette? Drink? You won't regret coming to us, sir. We're the oldest love-dispensing firm in the business, and much larger than our closest competitor, Passion Unlimited. Moreover, our fees are far more reasonable, and bring you an improved product. Might I ask how you heard of us? Did you see our full page ad in the Times? Or——"

"Joe sent me," Simon said.

"Ah, he's an active one," Mr. Tate said, shaking his head

playfully. "Well sir, there's no reason to delay. You've come a long way for love, and love you shall have." He reached for a button on his desk, but Simon stopped him.

Simon said, "I don't want to be rude or anything, but . . ."

"Yes?" Mr. Tate said, with an encouraging smile.

"I don't understand this," Simon blurted out, flushing deeply, beads of perspiration standing out on his forehead. "I think I'm in the wrong place. I didn't come all the way to Earth just for . . . I mean, you can't really sell *love*, can you? Not *love!* I mean, then it isn't really *love*, is it?"

"But of course!" Mr. Tate said, half rising from his chair in astonishment. "That's the whole point! Anyone can buy sex. Good lord, it's the cheapest thing in the universe, next to human life. But *love* is rare, *love* is special, *love* is found only on Earth. Have you read our brochure?"

"Bodies on a dark sea-beach?" Simon asked.

"Yes, that one. I wrote it. Gives something of the feeling, doesn't it? You can't get that feeling from just *anyone*, Mr. Simon. You can get that feeling only from someone who loves you."

Simon said dubiously, "It's not genuine love though, is it?"

"Of course it is! If we were selling simulated love, we'd label it as such. The advertising laws on Earth are strict, I can assure you. Anything can be sold, but it must be labelled properly. That's ethics, Mr. Simon!"

Tate caught his breath, and continued in a calmer tone. "No sir, make no mistake. Our product is not a substitute. It is the exact self-same feeling that poets and writers have raved about for thousands of years. Through the wonders of modern science we can bring this feeling to you at your convenience, attractively packaged, completely disposable, and for a ridiculously low price."

Simon said, "I pictured something more—spontaneous."

"Spontaneity has its charm," Mr. Tate agreed. "Our research labs are working on it. Believe me, there's nothing science can't produce, as long as there's a market for it."

"I don't like any of this," Simon said, getting to his feet. "I think I'll just go see a movie."

"Wait!" Mr. Tate cried. "You think we're trying to put something over on you. You think we'll introduce you to a girl who will *act* as though she loved you, but who in reality will not. Is that it?"

"I guess so," Simon said.

"But it just isn't so! It would be too costly for one thing.

For another, the wear and tear on the girl would be tremendous. And it would be psychologically unsound for her to attempt living a lie of such depth and scope."

"Then how do you do it?"

"By utilizing our understanding of science and the human mind."

To Simon, this sounded like double-talk. He moved toward the door.

"Tell me something," Mr. Tate said. "You're a bright looking young fellow. Don't you think you could tell real love from a counterfeit item?"

"Certainly."

"There's your safeguard! You must be satisfied, or don't pay us a cent."

"I'll think about it," Simon said.

"Why delay? Leading psychologists say that real love is a fortifier and a restorer of sanity, a balm for damaged egoes, a restorer of hormone balance, and an improver of the complexion. The love we supply you has everything: deep and abiding affection, unrestrained passion, complete faithfulness, an almost mystic affection for your defects as well as your virtues, a pitiful desire to please, and, as a plus that only Love Inc., can supply: that uncontrollable first spark, that blinding moment of love at first sight!"

Mr. Tate pressed a button. Simon frowned undecisively. The door opened, a girl stepped in, and Simon stopped thinking.

She was tall and slender, and her hair was brown with a sheen of red. Simon could have told you nothing about her face, except that it brought tears to his eyes. And if you asked him about her figure, he might have killed you.

"Miss Penny Bright," said Tate, "meet Mr. Alfred Simon."

The girl tried to speak but no words came, and Simon was equally dumbstruck. He looked at her and knew. Nothing else mattered. To the depths of his heart he knew that he was truly and completely loved.

They left at once, hand in hand, and were taken by jet to a small white cottage in a pine grove, overlooking the sea, and there they talked and laughed and loved, and later Simon saw his beloved wrapped in the sunset flame like a goddess of fire. And in blue twilight she looked at him with eyes enormous and dark, her known body mysterious again. The moon came up, bright and lunatic, changing flesh to shadow, and she wept and beat his chest with her small fists, and Simon wept too, although he did not know why. And at last dawn came, faint and disturbed, glimmering upon their parched lips and locked bodies, and nearby the booming surf deafened, inflamed, and maddened them.

At noon they were back in the offices of Love, Inc. Penny clutched his hand for a moment, then disappeared through an inner door.

"Was it real love?" Mr. Tate asked.

"Yes!"

"And was everything satisfactory?"

"Yes! It was love, it was the real thing! But why did she insist on returning?"

"Post-hypnotic command," Mr. Tate said.

"What?"

"What did you expect? Everyone wants love, but few wish to pay for it. Here is your bill, sir."

Simon paid, fuming. "This wasn't necessary," he said. "Of course I would pay you for bringing us together. Where is she now? What have you done with her?"

"Please," Mr. Tate said soothingly. "Try to calm yourself."

"I don't want to be calm!" Simon shouted. "I want Penny!"

"That will be impossible," Mr. Tate said, with the barest hint of frost in his voice. "Kindly stop making a spectacle of yourself."

"Are you trying to get more money out of me?" Simon shrieked. "All right, I'll pay. How much do I have to pay to get her out of your clutches?" And Simon yanked out his wallet and slammed it on the desk.

Mr. Tate poked the wallet with a stiffened forefinger. "Put that back in your pocket," he said. "We are an old and respectable firm. If you raise your voice again, I shall be forced to have you ejected."

Simon calmed himself with an effort, put the wallet back in his pocket and sat down. He took a deep breath and said, very quietly, "I'm sorry."

"That's better," Mr. Tate said. "I will not be shouted at. However, if you are reasonable, I can be reasonable too. Now, what's the trouble?"

"The trouble?" Simon's voice started to lift. He controlled it and said, "She loves me."

"Of course."

"Then how can you separate us?"

"What has the one thing got to do with the other?" Mr.

Tate asked. "Love is a delightful interlude, a relaxation, good for the intellect, for the ego, for the hormone balance, and for the skin tone. But one would hardly wish to continue loving, would one?"

"I would," Simon said. "This love was special, unique——"

"They all are," Mr. Tate said. "But as you know, they are all produced in the same way."

"What?"

"Surely you know something about the mechanics of love production?"

"No," Simon said. "I thought it was—natural."

Mr. Tate shook his head. "We gave up natural selection centuries ago, shortly after the Mechanical Revolution. It was too slow, and commercially unfeasible. Why bother with it, when we can produce any feeling at will by conditioning and proper stimulation of certain brain centers? The result? Penny, completely in love with you! Your own bias, which we calculated, in favor of her particular somatotype, made it complete. We always throw in the dark sea-beach, the lunatic moon, the pallid dawn——"

"Then she could have been made to love anyone," Simon said slowly.

"Could have been brought to love anyone," Mr. Tate corrected.

"Oh, lord, how did she get into this horrible work?" Simon asked.

"She came in and signed a contract in the usual way," Tate said. "It pays very well. And at the termination of the lease, we return her original personality—untouched! But why do you call the work horrible? There's nothing reprehensible about love."

"It wasn't love!" Simon cried.

"But it was! The genuine article! Unbiased scientific firms have made qualitative tests of it, in comparison with the natural thing. In every case, our love tested out to more depth, passion, fervor and scope."

Simon shut his eyes tightly, opened them and said, "Listen to me. I don't care about your scientific tests. I love her, she loves me, that's all that counts. Let me speak to her! I want to marry her!"

Mr. Tate wrinkled his nose in distaste. "Come, come, man! You wouldn't want to marry a girl like that! But if it's marriage you're after, we deal in that, too. I can arrange an idyllic and nearly spontaneous love-match for you with a guaranteed government-inspected virgin——"

"No! I love Penny! At least let me speak to her!"

"That will be quite impossible," Mr. Tate said.

"Why?"

Mr. Tate pushed a button on his desk. "Why do you think? We've wiped out the previous indoctrination. Penny is now in love with someone else."

And then Simon understood. He had realized that even now Penny was looking at another man with that passion he had known, feeling for another man that complete and bottomless love that unbiased scientific firms had shown to be so much greater than the old-fashioned, commercially unfeasible natural selection, and that upon that same dark sea-beach mentioned in the advertising brochure——

He lunged for Tate's throat. Two attendants, who had entered the office a few moments earlier, caught him and led him to the door.

"Remember!" Tate called. "This in no way invalidates your own experience."

Hellishly enough, Simon knew that what Tate said was true.

And then he found himself on the street.

At first, all he desired was to escape from Earth, where the commercial impracticalities were more than a normal man could afford. He walked very quickly, and his Penny walked beside him, her face glorified with love for him, and him, and him, and you, and you.

And of course he came to the shooting gallery.

"Try your luck?" the manager asked.

"Set 'em up," said Alfred Simon.

ALL THE THINGS
YOU ARE

There are regulations to govern the conduct of First Contact spaceships, rules drawn up in desperation and followed in despair, for what rule can predict the effect of any action upon the mentality of an alien people?

Jan Maarten was gloomily pondering this as he came into the atmosphere of Durell IV. He was a big, middle-aged man with thin ash-blond hair and a round worried face. Long ago, he had concluded that almost any rule was better than none. Therefore he followed his meticulously, but with an ever-present sense of uncertainty and human fallibility.

These were ideal qualications for the job of First Contacter.

He circled the planet, low enough for observation, but not too low, since he didn't want to frighten the inhabitants. He noted the signs of a primitive-pastoral civilization and tried to remember everything he had learned in Volume 4, *Projected Techniques for First Contact on So-called Primitive-pastoral Worlds*, published by the Department of Alien Psychology. Then he brought the ship down on a rocky, grass-covered plain, near a typical medium-sized village, but not too near, using the Silent Sam landing technique.

"Prettily done," commented Croswell, his assistant, who was too young to be bothered by uncertainties.

Chedka, the Eborian linguist, said nothing. He was sleeping, as usual.

Maarten grunted something and went to the rear of the ship to run his tests. Croswell took up his post at the viewport.

"Here they come," Croswell reported half an hour later. "About a dozen of them, definitely humanoidal." Upon closer inspection, he saw that the natives of Durell were flabby, dead-white in coloration and deadpan in expression. Croswell hesitated, then added, "They're not too handsome."

"What are they doing?" Maarten asked.

"Just looking us over," Croswell said. He was a slender young man with an unusually large and lustrous mustache which he had grown on the long journey out from Terra. He stroked it with the pride of a man who has been able to raise a really good mustache.

"They're about twenty yards from the ship now," Croswell reported. He leaned forward, flattening his nose ludicrously against the port, which was constructed of one-way glass.

Croswell could look out, but no one could look in. The Department of Alien Psychology had ordered the change last year, after a Department ship had botched a first contact on Carella II. The Carellans had stared into the ship, become alarmed at something within, and fled. The Department still didn't know what had alarmed them, for a second contact had never been successfully established.

That mistake would never happen again.

"What now?" Maarten called.

"One of them's coming forward alone. Chief, perhaps. Or sacrificial offering."

"What is he wearing?"

"He has on a—a sort of—will you kindly come here and look for yourself?"

Maarten, at his instrument bank, had been assembling a sketchy picture of Durell. The planet had a breathable atmosphere, an equitable climate, and gravity comparable to that of Earth. It had valuable deposits of radioactives and rare metals. Best of all, it tested free of the virulent microorganisms and poisonous vapors which tended to make a Contacter's life feverishly short.

Durell was going to be a valuable neighbor to Earth, provided the natives were friendly—and the Contacters skillful.

Maarten walked to the viewport and studied the natives. "They are wearing pastel clothing. We shall wear pastel clothing.

"Check," said Croswell.

"They are unarmed. We shall go unarmed."

"Roger."

"They are wearing sandals. We shall wear sandals as well."

"To hear is to obey."

"I notice they have no facial hair," Maarten said, with the barest hint of a smile. "I'm sorry, Ed, but that mustache—"

"Not my mustache!" Croswell yelped, quickly putting a protective hand over it.

"I'm afraid so."

"But, Jan, I've been six months raising it!"

"It has to go. That should be obvious."

"I don't see why," Croswell said indignantly.

"Because first impressions are *vital*. When an unfavorable first impression has been made, subsequent contacts become difficult, sometimes impossible. Since we know nothing about these people, conformity is our safest course. We try to look like them, dress in colors that are pleasing, or at least acceptable to them, copy their gestures, interact within their framework of acceptance in every way—"

"All right, all right," Croswell said. "I suppose I can grow another on the way back."

They looked at each other; then both began laughing. Croswell had lost three mustaches in this manner.

While Croswell shaved, Maarten stirred their linguist into wakefulness. Chedka was a lemurlike humanoid from Eboria IV, one of the few planets where Earth maintained successful relations. The Eborians were natural linguists, aided by the kind of associative ability found in nuisances who supply words in conversation—only the Eborians were always right. They had wandered over a considerable portion of the Galaxy in their time and might have attained quite a place in it were it not that they needed twenty hours' sleep out of twenty-four.

Croswell finished shaving and dressed in pale green coveralls and sandals. All three stepped through the degermifier. Maarten took a deep breath, uttered a silent prayer and opened the port.

A low sigh went up from the crowd of Durellans, although the chief—or sacrifice—was silent. They were indeed humanlike, if one overlooked their pallor and the gentle sheeplike blandness of their features—features upon which Maarten could read no trace of expression.

"Don't use any facial contortions," Maarten warned Croswell.

Slowly they advanced until they were ten feet from the leading Durellan. Then Maarten said in a low voice, "We come in peace."

Chedka translated, then listened to the answer, which was so soft as to be almost undecipherable.

"Chief says welcome," Chedka reported in his economical English.

"Good, good," Maarten said. He took a few more steps forward and began to speak, pausing every now and then for translation. Earnestly, and with extreme conviction, he intoned Primary Speech BB-32 (for humanoid, primitive-pastoral, tentatively non-aggressive aliens).

Even Croswell, who was impressed by very little, had to admit it was a fine speech. Maarten said they were wanderers from afar, come out of the Great Nothingness to engage in friendly discourse with the gentle people of Durell. He spoke of green and distant Earth, so like this planet, and of the fine and humble people of Earth who stretched out hands in greeting. He told of the great spirit of peace and cooperation that emanated from Earth, of universal friendship, and many other excellent things.

Finally he was done. There was a long silence.

"Did he understand it all?" Maarten whispered to Chedka.

The Eborian nodded, waiting for the chief's reply. Maarten was perspiring from the exertion and Croswell couldn't stop nervously fingering his newly shaven upper lip.

The chief opened his mouth, gasped, made a little half turn, and collapsed to the ground.

It was an embarrassing moment and one uncovered by any amount of theory.

The chief didn't rise; apparently it was not a ceremonial fall. As a matter of fact, his breathing seemed labored, like that of a man in a coma.

Under the circumstances, the Contact team could only retreat to their ship and await further developments.

Half an hour later, a native approached the ship and conversed with Chedka, keeping a wary eye on the Earthmen and departing immediately.

"What did he say?" Croswell asked.

"Chief Moréri apologizes for fainting," Chedka told them. "He said it was inexcusably bad manners."

"Ah!" Maarten exclaimed. "His fainting might help us, after all—make him eager to repair his 'impoliteness.' Just as long as it was a fortuitous circumstance, unrelated to us—"

"Not," Chedka said.

"Not what?"

"Not unrelated," the Eborian said, curling up and going to sleep.

Maarten shook the little linguist awake. "What else did the chief say? How was his fainting related to us?"

Chedka yawned copiously. "The chief was very embarrassed. He faced the wind from your mouth as long as he could, but the alien odor—"

"My breath?" Maarten asked. "My breath knocked him out?"

Chedka nodded, giggled unexpectedly and went to sleep.

Evening came, and the long dim twilight of Durell merged imperceptibly into night. In the village, cooking fires glinted through the surrounding forest and winked out one by one. But lights burned within the spaceship until dawn. And when the sun rose, Chedka slipped out of the ship on a mission into the village. Croswell brooded over his morning coffee, while Maarten rummaged through the ship's medicine chest.

"It's purely a temporary setback," Croswell was saying hopefully. "Little things like this are bound to happen. Remember that time on Dingoforeaba VI—"

"It's little things that close planets forever," Maarten said.

"But how could anyone possibly guess—"

"I should have foreseen it," Maarten growled angrily. "Just because our breath hasn't been offensive anywhere else—here it is!"

Triumphantly he held up a bottle of pink tablets. "Absolutely guaranteed to neutralize any breath, even that of a hyena. Have a couple."

Croswell accepted the pills. "Now what?"

"Now we wait until—aha! What did he say?"

Chedka slipped through the entry port, rubbing his eyes. "The chief apologizes for fainting."

"We know that. What else?"

"He welcomes you to the village of Lannit at your convenience. The chief feels that this incident shouldn't alter the course of friendship between two peace-loving courteous peoples."

Maarten sighed with relief. He cleared his throat and asked hesitantly, "Did you mention to him about the forthcoming —ah—improvement in our breaths?"

"I assured him it would be corrected," Chedka said, "although it never bothered me."

"Fine, fine. We will leave for the village now. Perhaps you should take one of these pills?"

"There's nothing wrong with my breath," the Eborian said complacently.

They set out at once for the village of Lannit.

When one deals with a primitive-pastoral people, one looks for simple but highly symbolic gestures, since that is what they understand best. Imagery! Clear-cut and decisive parallels! Few words but many gestures! Those were the rules in dealing with primitive-pastorals.

As Maarten approached the village, a natural and highly symbolic ceremony presented itself. The natives were waiting in their village, which was in a clearing in the forest. Separating forest from village was a dry stream bed, and across that bed was a small stone bridge.

Maarten advanced to the center of the bridge and stopped, beaming benignly on the Durellans. When he saw several of them shudder and turn away, he smoothed out his features, remembering his own injunction on facial contortions. He paused for a long moment.

"What's up?" Croswell asked, stopping in front of the bridge.

In a loud voice, Maarten cried, "Let this bridge symbolize the link, now eternally forged, that joins this beautiful planet with—" Croswell called out a warning, but Maarten didn't know what was wrong. He stared at the villagers; they had made no movement.

"Get off the bridge!" Croswell shouted. But before Maarten could move, the entire structure had collapsed under him and he fell bone-shakingly into the dry stream.

"Damnedest thing I ever saw," Croswell said, helping him to his feet. "As soon as you raised your voice, that stone began to pulverize. Sympathetic vibration, I imagine."

Now Maarten understood why the Durellans spoke in whispers. He struggled to his feet, then groaned and sat down again.

"What's wrong?" Croswell asked.

"I seem to have wrenched my ankle," Maarten said miserably.

Chief Moréri came up, followed by twenty or so villagers, made a short speech and presented Maarten with a walking stick of carved and polished black wood.

"Thanks," Maarten muttered, standing up and leaning gingerly on the cane. "What did he say?" he asked Chedka.

"The chief said that the bridge was only a hundred years old and in good repair," Chedka translated. "He apologizes that his ancestors didn't build it better."

"Hmm," Maarten said.

"And the chief says that you are probably an unlucky man."

He might be right, Maarten thought. Or perhaps Earthmen were just a fumbling race. For all their good intentions, population after population feared them, hated them, envied them, mainly on the basis of unfavorable first impressions.

Still, there seemed to be a chance here. What else could go wrong?

Forcing a smile, then quickly erasing it, Maarten limped into the village beside Moréri.

Technologically, the Durellan civilization was of a low order. A limited use had been made of wheel and lever, but the concept of mechanical advantage had been carried no further. There was evidence of a rudimentary knowledge of plane geometry and a fair idea of astronomy.

Artistically, however, the Durellans were adept and surprisingly sophisticated, particularly in wood carving. Even the simplest huts had bas-relief panels, beautifully conceived and executed.

"Do you think I could take some photographs?" Croswell asked.

"I see no reason why not," Maarten said. He ran his fingers lovingly over a large panel, carved of the same straight-grained black wood that formed his cane. The finish was as smooth as skin beneath his fingertips.

The chief gave his approval and Croswell tooks photographs and tracings of Durellan home, market and temple decorations.

Maarten wandered around, gently touching the intricate bas-reliefs, speaking with some of the natives through Chedka, and generally sorting out his impressions.

The Durrellans, Maarten judged, were highly intelligent and had a potential comparable to that of *Homo sapiens*. Their lack of a defined technology was more the expression of a cooperation with nature rather than a flaw in their makeup. They seemed inherently peace-loving and non-aggressive—valuable neighbors for an Earth that, after centuries of confusion, was striving toward a similar goal.

This was going to be the basis of his report to the Second Contact Team. With it, he hoped to be able to add, *A favorable impression seems to have been left concerning Earth. No unusual difficulties are to be expected.*

Chedka had been talking earnestly with Chief Moréri. Now, looking slightly more wide awake than usual, he came over and conferred with Maarten in a hushed voice. Maarten nodded, keeping his face expressionless, and went over to Croswell, who was snapping his last photographs.

"All ready for the big show?" Maarten asked.

"What show?"

"Moréri is throwing a feast for us tonight," Maarten said. "Very big, very important feast. A final gesture of good will and all that." Although his tone was casual, there was a gleam of deep satisfaction in his eyes.

Croswell's reaction was more immediate. "Then we've made it! The contact is successful!"

Behind him, two natives shook at the loudness of his voice and tottered feebly away.

"We've made it," Maarten whispered, "if we watch our step. They're a fine, understanding people—but we do seem to grate on them a bit."

By evening, Maarten and Croswell had completed a chemical examination of the Durellan foods and found nothing harmful to humans. They took several more pink tablets, changed coveralls and sandals, bathed again in the degermifier, and proceeded to the feast.

The first course was an orange-green vegetable that tasted like squash. Then Chief Moréri gave a short talk on the importance of intercultural relations. They were served a dish resembling rabbit and Croswell was called upon to give a speech.

"Remember," Maarten whispered, "*whisper!*"

Croswell stood up and began to speak. Keeping his voice down and his face blank, he began to enumerate the many similarities between Earth and Durell, depending mainly on gestures to convey his message.

Chedka translated. Maarten nodded his approval. The chief nodded. The feasters nodded.

Croswell made his last points and sat down. Maarten clapped him on the shoulder. "Well done, Ed. You've got a natural gift for—what's wrong?"

Croswell had a startled and incredulous look on his face. "Look!"

Maarten turned. The chief and the feasters, their eyes open and staring, were still nodding.

"Chedka!" Maarten whispered. "Speak to them!"

The Eborian asked the chief a question. There was no response. The chief continued his rhythmic nodding.

"Those gestures!" Maarten said. "You must have hypnotized them!" He scratched his head, then coughed once, loudly. The Durellans stopped nodding, blinked their eyes and began to talk rapidly and nervously among themselves.

"They say you've got some strong powers," Chedka translated at random. "They say that aliens are pretty queer people and doubt if they can be trusted."

"What does the chief say?" Maarten asked.

"The chief believes you're all right. He is telling them that you meant no harm."

"Good enough. Let's stop while we're ahead."

He stood up, followed by Croswell and Chedka.

"We are leaving now," he told the chief in a whisper, "but we beg permission for others of our kind to visit you. Forgive the mistakes we have made; they were due only to ignorance of your ways."

Chedka translated, and Maarten went on whispering, his face expressionless, his hands at his sides. He spoke of the oneness of the Galaxy, the joys of cooperation, peace, the exchange of goods and art, and the essential solidarity of all human life.

Moréri, though still a little dazed from the hypnotic experience, answered that the Earthmen would always be welcome.

Impulsively, Croswell held out his hand. The chief looked at it for a moment, puzzled, then took it, obviously wondering what to do with it and why.

He gasped in agony and pulled his hand back. They could see deep burns blotched red against his skin.

"What could have—"

"Perspiration!" Maarten said. "It's an acid. Must have an almost instantaneous effect upon their particular makeup. Let's get out of here."

The natives were milling together and they had picked up some stones and pieces of wood. The chief, although still in pain, was arguing with them, but the Earthmen didn't wait to hear the results of the discussion. They retreated to their ship, as fast as Maarten could hobble with the help of his cane.

The forest was dark behind them and filled with suspicious movements. Out of breath, they arrived at the spaceship. Croswell, in the lead, sprawled over a tangle of grass and fell head-first against the port with a resounding clang.

"Damn!" he howled in pain.

The ground rumbled beneath them, began to tremble and slide away.

"Into the ship!" Maarten ordered.

They managed to take off before the ground gave way completely.

"It must have been sympathetic vibration again," Croswell said, several hours later, when the ship was in space. "But of all the luck—to be perched on a rock fault!"

Maarten sighed and shook his head. "I really don't know what to do. I'd like to go back, explain to them but—"

"We've outlived our welcome," Croswell said.

"Apparently. Blunders, nothing but blunders. We started out badly, and everything we did made it worse."

"It is not what you *do*," Chedka explained in the most sympathetic voice they had ever heard him use. "It's not your fault. It's what you *are*."

Maarten considered that for a moment. "Yes, you're right. Our voices shatter their land, our expressions disgust them, our gestures hypnotize them, our breath asphyxiates them, our perspiration burns them. Oh, Lord!"

"Lord, Lord," Croswell agreed glumly. "We're living chemical factories—only turning out poison gas and corrosives exclusively."

"But that is not *all* you are," Chedka said. "Look."

He held up Maarten's walking stick. Along the upper part, where Maarten had handled it, long-dormant buds had burst into pink and white flowers, and their scent filled the cabin.

"You see?" Chedka said. "You are *this*, also."

"That stick was dead," Croswell mused. "Some oil in our skin, I imagine."

Maarten shuddered. "Do you suppose that all the carvings we touched—the huts—the temple—"

"I should think so," Croswell said.

Maarten closed his eyes and visualized it, the sudden bursting into bloom of the dead, dried wood.

"I think they'll understand," he said, trying very hard to believe himself. "It's a pretty symbol and they're quite an understanding people. I think they'll approve of—well, at least some of the things we are."

TRAP

Samish, I am in some need of assistance. The situation is potentially dangerous, so come at once.

It shows how right you were, Samish, old friend. I should never have trusted a Terran. They are a sly, ignorant, irresponsible race, just as you have always pointed out.

Nor are they as stupid as they seem. I am beginning to believe that the slenderness of the tentacle is not the only criterion of intelligence.

What a sorry mess, Samish! And the plan seemed so foolproof . . .

Ed Dailey saw a gleam of metal outside his cabin door, but he was still too sleepy to investigate.

He had awakened shortly after daybreak and tiptoed outside for a glimpse at the weather. It was unpromising. There had been a heavy rain during the night and water dripped from every leaf and branch of the surrounding forest. His station wagon had a drowned look and the dirt road leading up the mountainside was a foot-thick in mud.

His friend Thurston came to the door in pajamas, his round face flushed with sleep and Buddhalike in its placidity.

"It always rains on the first day of a vacation," Thurston stated. "Rule of nature."

"Might be a good day for trout," Dailey said.

"It might. But it is a better day for building a roaring fire in the fireplace and drinking hot buttered rum."

For eleven years, they had been taking a short autumn vacation together, but for different reasons.

Dailey had a romantic love for equipment. The clerks in New York's fancier sports shops hung expensive parkas on his high, stooped shoulders, parkas such as one would wear on the trail of the Abominable Snowman in the fastnesses of Tibet. They sold him ingenious little stoves that would burn through a hurricane and wickedly curved knives of the best Swedish steel.

Dailey loved to feel a lean canteen against his side and a blued-steel rifle over his shoulder. But the canteen usually contained rum and the rifle was used against nothing deadlier than tin cans. For in spite of his dreams, Dailey was a friendly man, with no malice toward bird or beast.

His friend Thurston was overweight and short of wind, and burdened himself only with the lightest of fly rods and the smallest of shotguns. By the second week, he usually managed to steer the hunt to Lake Placid, to the cocktail lounges that were his true environment. There, with an incredible knowledge of spoor and lair, he placidly hunted the pretty vacationing girls instead of the brown bear, the black bear, or the mountain deer.

This mild exercise was more than adequate for two soft and successful businessmen on the wrong side of forty, and they returned to the city tanned and refreshed, with a new lease on life and a renewed tolerance for their wives.

"Rum it is," Daily said. "What's that?" He had noticed the gleam of metal near the cabin.

Thurston walked over and poked the object with his foot. "Odd-looking thing."

Dailey parted the grass and saw an open framework box about four feet square, constructed of metal strips, and hinged on top. Written boldly on one of the strips was the single word TRAP.

"Where did you buy *that?*" Thurston asked.

"I didn't." Dailey found a plastic tag attached to one of the metal strips. He pulled it loose and read: "Dear Friend, this is a new and revolutionary design in a TRAP. To introduce the TRAP to the general public, we are giving you this model *absolutely free!* You will find it a unique and valuable device for the capture of small game, provided you follow *precisely* the directions on the other side. Good luck and good hunting!"

"If this isn't the strangest thing," Dailey said. "Do you suppose it was left during the night?"

"Who cares?" Thurston shrugged. "My stomach is rumbling. Let's make breakfast."

"Aren't you interested in this?"

"Not particularly. It's just another gadget. You've got a hundred like it. That bear trap from Abercrombie and Fitch. The jaguar horn from Battler's. The crocodile lure from—"

"I've never seen a trap like this," Dailey mused. "Pretty clever advertising, just to leave it here."

"They'll bill you for it eventually," Thurston said cynically. "I'm going to make breakfast. You'll wash the dishes."

He went inside while Dailey turned the tag over and read the other side.

"Take the TRAP to a clearing and anchor it to any convenient TREE with the attached chain. Press Button One on the base. This primes the TRAP. Wait five seconds and press Button Two. This activates the TRAP. Nothing more is required until a CAPTURE has been effected. Then press Button Three to deactivate and open the TRAP, and remove the PREY.

"Warning! Keep the TRAP closed at all times except when removing the PREY. No opening is required for the PREY'S ingress, since the TRAP works on the principle of Osmotic Section and inducts the PREY directly into the TRAP."

"What won't they think of next?" Dailey said admiringly.

"Breakfast is ready," Thurston called.

"First help me set the trap."

Thurston, dressed now in Bermuda shorts and a loud sport shirt, came out and peered at the trap dubiously. "Do you really think we should fool with it?"

"Of course. Maybe we can catch a fox."

"What on Earth would we do with a fox?" Thurston demanded.

"Turn it loose," Dailey said. "The fun is in the catching. Here, help me lift it."

The trap was surprisingly heavy. Together they dragged it fifty yards from the cabin and tied the chain to a young pine tree. Dailey pushed the first button and the trap glowed faintly. Thurston backed away anxiously.

After five seconds, Dailey pressed the second button.

The forest dripped and squirrels chattered in the treetops and the long grass rustled faintly. The trap lay quietly beside the tree, its open metal framework glowing faintly.

"Come in," Thurston said. "The eggs are undoubtedly cold."

Dailey followed him back to the cabin, glancing over his shoulder at the trap. It lay in the forest, silent and waiting.

Samish, where are you? My need is becoming increasingly urgent. Unbelievable as it will sound, my little planetoid is being pulled apart before my very eyes! You are my oldest friend, Samish, the companion of my youth, the best man at my mating, and a friend of Fregl as well. I'm counting on you. Don't delay too long.

I have already beamed you the beginning of my story. The Terrans accepted my trap as a trap, nothing more. And they began to use it at once, with no thought to the possible consequences. I had counted on this. The fantastic curiosity of the Terran species is well known.

During this period, my wife was crawling gaily around the planetoid, redecorating our hutch and enjoying the change from city life. Everything was going well. . . .

During breakfast, Thurston explained in pedantic detail why a trap could not function unless it had an opening to admit the prey. Dailey smiled and spoke of osmotic section. Thurston insisted that there was no such thing. When the dishes were washed and dried, they walked over the wet, springy grass to the trap.

"Look!" Dailey shouted.

Something was in the trap, something about the size of a rabbit, but colored a bright green. Its eyes were extended on stalks and it clicked lobsterlike claws at them.

"No more rum before breakfast," Thurston said. "Starting tomorrow. Hand me the canteen."

Dailey gave it to him and Thurston poured down a generous double shot. Then he looked at the trapped creature again and went, "Brr!"

"I think it's a new species," Dailey said.

"New species of nightmare. Can't we just go to Lake Placid and forget about it?"

"No, of course not. I've never seen anything like this in my zoology books. It could be completely unknown to science. What will we keep it in?"

"Keep it in?"

"Well, certainly. It can't stay in the trap. We'll have to build a cage and then find out what it eats."

Thurston's face lost some of its habitual serenity. "Now look here, Ed. I'm not sharing my vacation with anything like that. It's probably poisonous. I'm sure it has dirty habits." He took a deep breath and continued. "There's something unnatural about that trap. It's—inhuman!"

Dailey grinned. "I'm sure they said that about Ford's first car and Edison's incandescent lamp. This trap is just another example of American progress and know-how."

"I'm all for progress," Thurston stated firmly, "but in other directions. Can't we just—"

He looked at his friend's face and stopped talking. Dailey had an expression that Cortez might have worn as he approached the summit of a peak in Darien.

"Yes," Dailey said after a while. "I think so."

"What?"

"Tell you later. First let's build a cage and set the trap again."

Thurston groaned, but followed him.

Why haven't you come yet, Samish? Don't you appreciate the seriousness of my situation? Haven't I made it clear how much depends upon you? Think of your old friend! Think of the lustrous-skinned Fregl, for whose sake I got into this mess. Communicate with me, at least.

The Terrans used the trap, which, of course, was not a trap at all, but a matter transmitter. I had the other end concealed on the planetoid, and fed into it three small animals which I found in the garden. The Terrans removed them from the transmitter each time—for what purpose, I couldn't guess. But a Terran will keep anything.

After the third beast passed through and had not been returned, I knew that all was in readiness.

So I prepared for the fourth and final sending, the all-important one, for which all else was mere preparation.

They were standing in the low shed attached to their cabin. Thurston looked with distaste at the three cages made of heavy mosquito netting. Inside each cage was a creature.

"Ugh," Thurston said. "They smell."

In the first cage was the original capture, the stalk-eyed, lobster-clawed beast. Next came a bird with three sets of scaly wings. Finally there was something that looked like a snake, except that it had a head at each end.

Within the cages were bowls of milk, plates of minced meat, vegetables, grasses, bark—all untouched.

"They just won't eat anything," Dailey said.

"Obviously they're sick," Thurston told him. "Probably germ carriers. Can't we get rid of them, Ed?"

Dailey looked squarely at his friend. "Tom, have you ever desired fame?"

"What?"

"Fame. The knowledge that your name will go down through the ages."

"I am a businessman," Thurston said. "I never considered the possibility."

"Never?"

Thurston smiled foolishly. "Well, what man hasn't? What did you have in mind?"

"These creatures," Dailey said, "are unique. We will present them to a museum."

"Ah?" Thurston queried interestedly.

"The Dailey-Thurston exhibit of creatures hitherto unknown."

"They might name the species after us," Thurston said. "After all, we discovered them."

"Of course they would! Our names would go down with Livingstone, Audubon and Teddy Roosevelt."

"Hmm." Thurston thought deeply. "I suppose the Museum of Natural History would be the place. I'm sure they'd arrange an exhibit—"

"I wasn't thinking merely in terms of an exhibit," Dailey said. "I was thinking more of a wing—the Dailey-Thurston Wing."

Thurston looked at his friend in amazement. There were depths to Dailey that he had never imagined. "But, Ed, we have only three of them. We can't equip a wing with three exhibits."

"There must be more where these came from. Let's examine the trap."

This time the trap contained a creature almost three feet tall, with a small green head and a forked tail. It had at least a dozen thick cilia, all of them waving furiously.

"The rest were quiet," Thurston said apprehensively. "Maybe this one is dangerous."

"We will handle it with nets," Dailey replied decisively. "And then I want to get in touch with the museum."

After considerable work, they transferred the thing to a cage. The trap was reset and Dailey sent the following wire to the Museum of Natural History: HAVE DISCOVERED AT LEAST FOUR ANIMALS WHICH I SUSPECT TO BE NEW SPECIES STOP HAVE YOU ROOM FOR SUITABLE EXHIBIT STOP BETTER SEND A MAN UP AT ONCE.

Then, at Thurston's insistence, he wired several impeccable character references to the museum, so they wouldn't think he was a crank.

That afternoon, Dailey explained his theory to Thurston. There was, he felt sure, a primeval pocket isolated in this section of the Adirondacks. Within it were creatures which had survived from prehistoric times. They had never been captured because, due to their great antiquity, they had acquired a high degree of experience and caution. But the trap—operating on the new principle of osmotic section—had proved to be beyond their experience.

"The Adirondacks have been pretty well explored," Thurston objected.

"Not well enough, apparently," Dailey said, with irrefutable logic.

Later, they returned to the trap. It was empty.

I can just barely hear you, Samish. Kindly step up the volume. Or, better still, get here in person. What's the use of beaming me, in the spot I'm in? The situation is steadily becoming more and more desperate.

What, Samish? The rest of the story? It's obvious enough. After three animals had passed through the transmitter, I knew I was ready. Now was the time to tell my wife.

Accordingly, I asked her to crawl into the garden with me. She was quite pleased.

"Tell me, my dear," she said, "has something been bothering you of late?"

"Um," said I.

"Have I displeased you?" she asked.

"No, sweetheart," I said. "You have tried your best, but it just isn't good enough. I am going to take a new mate."

She stood motionless, her cilia swaying in confusion. Then she exclaimed, "Fregl!"

"Yes," I told her, "the glorious Fregl has consented to share my hutch."

"But you forget we were mated for life."

"I know. A pity you insisted on that formality." And with one clever shove, I pushed her into the matter transmitter.

Samish, you should have seen her expression! Her cilia writhed, she screamed, and was gone.

I was free at last! A little nauseous, but free! Free to mate with the splendid Fregl!

Now you can appreciate the full perfection of the scheme. It was necessary to secure the Terrans' cooperation, since a matter transmitter must be manipulated from both ends. I had disguised it as a trap, because Terrans will believe anything. And as my master stroke, I sent them my wife.

Let them try to live with her! I never could!

Foolproof, absolutely foolproof. My wife's body would never

turn up, because the acquisitive. Terrans keep what they get. No one could ever prove anything.

And then, Samish, then it happened. . . .

The cabin's air of rustic serenity was gone. Tire tracks crossed and recrossed the muddy road. The grounds were littered with flash bulbs, empty cigarette packs, candy wrappers, pencil stubs and bits of paper. But now, after a hectic few hours, everyone was gone. Only a sour taste remained.

Dailey and Thurston stood beside the empty trap, staring hopelessly at it.

"What do you suppose is wrong with the damned thing?" Dailey asked, giving the trap a frustrated kick.

"Maybe there's nothing else to capture," Thurston suggested.

"There has to be! Why would it take four completely alien beasts and then no more?" He knelt beside the trap and said bitterly, "Those stupid museum people! And those reporters!"

"In a way," Thurston said cautiously, "you can't blame them—"

"Can't I? Accusing me of a *hoax!* Did you hear them, Tom? They asked me how I performed the *skin grafts!*"

"It's too bad the animals were all dead by the time the museum people got here," Thurston said. "That did look suspicious."

"The idiotic creatures wouldn't eat. Was that my fault? And those newspaper people . . . Really, you would think the metropolitan newspapers would hire more intelligent reporters."

"You shouldn't have promised to capture more animals," Thurston said. "It was when the trap didn't produce that they suspected a hoax."

"Of course I promised! How should I guess the trap would stop with that fourth capture? And why did they laugh when I told them about the osmotic section system of capture?"

"They never heard of it," Thurston answered wearily. "No one ever heard of it. Let's go to Lake Placid and forget the whole thing."

"No! This thing must work again. It must!" Dailey primed and activated the trap and stared at it for several seconds. Then he opened the hinged top.

Dailey stuck his hand into the trap and let out a scream. "My hand! It's gone!" He leaped backward.

"No, it's not," Thurston assured him.

Dailey examined both hands, rubbed them together and insisted, "My hand disappeared inside that trap."

"Now, now," Thurston said soothingly. "A little rest in Lake Placid will do you a world of good—"

Dailey stood over the trap and pushed in his hand. It disappeared. He reacher farther in and watched his arm vanish up to the shoulder. He looked at Thurston with a smile of triumph.

"Now I see how it works," he said. "Those animals didn't come from the Adirondacks at all!"

"Where did they come from?"

"From wherever my hand is! Want more, do they? Call me a liar? I'll show them!"

"Ed! Don't do it! You don't know what—"

But Dailey had already stepped feet-first into the trap. His feet disappeared. Slowly he lowered his body until only his head was visible.

"Wish me luck," he said.

"Ed!"

Dailey held his nose and plunged out of sight.

Samish, if you don't come immediately, it will be too late! I must stop beaming you. The enormous Terran has completely ransacked my little planetoid. He has shoved everything, living or dead, through the transmitter. My home is in ruins.

And now he is tearing down my hutch! Samish, this monster means to capture me as a specimen! There's no time to lose!

Samish, what can be keeping you? You, my oldest friend . . .

What, Samish? What are you saying? You can't mean it! Not you and Fregl! Reconsider, old friend! Remember our friendship!

THE
BODY

When Professor Meyer opened his eyes he saw, leaning anxiously over him, three of the young specialists who had performed the operation. It struck him at once that they would have to be young to attempt what they had attempted; young and irreverent, possessed of encyclopedic technical knowledge to the exclusion of all else; iron-nerved, steel-fingered, inhuman, in fact. They had the qualifications of automatons.

He was so struck by this bit of post-anesthetic reasoning that it took him a moment to realize that the operation had been a success.

"How do you feel, sir?"

"Are you all right?"

"Can you speak, sir? If not, just nod your head. Or blink."

They watched anxiously.

Professor Meyer gulped, testing the limitations of his new palate, tongue and throat. Then he said, very thickly, "I think —I think—"

"He's all right!" Cassidy shouted. "Feldman! Wake up!"

Feldman leaped up from the spare cot and fumbled for his glasses. "He's up so soon? Did he speak?"

"Yes, he spoke! He spoke like an angel! We finally made it, Freddie!"

Feldman found his glasses and rushed to the operating table. "Could you say something else, sir? Anything?"

"I am—I am—"

"Oh, God," Feldman said. "I think I'm going to faint."

The three men burst into laughter. They surrounded Feldman and slapped him on the back. Feldman began to laugh, too, but soon he was coughing violently.

"Where's Kent?" Cassidy shouted. "He should be here, damn it. He kept that damned ossilyscope on the line for ten solid hours. Steadiest thing I ever saw. Where the devil is he?"

"He went after sandwiches," Lupowicz said. "Here he comes. Kent, Kent, we made it!"

Kent came through the door carrying two paper bags, with

half a sandwich thrust in his mouth. He swallowed convul-
sively. "Did he speak? What did he say?"

Behind Kent, there was an uproar. A dozen men rushed
toward the door.

"Get them out of here!" Feldman screamed. "They can't
interview him tonight. Where's that cop?"

A policeman pushed his way through and blocked the door.
"You heard what the docs said, boys."

"This isn't fair. This Meyer, he belongs to the world."

"What were his first words?"

"What did he say?"

"Did you really change him into a dog?"

"What kind of dog?"

"Can he wag his tail?"

"He said he was fine," the policeman told them, blocking
the door. "Come on now, boys."

A photographer ducked under the policeman's arm. He
looked at Professor Meyer on the operating table and muttered, "Jesus!" He raised his camera. "Look up, boy—"

Kent put his hand over the lens as the flashgun popped.

"Whatdja do that for?" the photographer asked.

"You now have a picture of Kent's hand," Kent said with
sarcasm. "Enlarge it, and hang it in the Museum of Modern
Art. Now get out of here before I break your neck."

"Come on, boys," the policeman repeated sternly, herding
the newsmen away. He turned back and glanced at Professor
Meyer on the operating table. "Jesus! I still can't believe it!"
he muttered, and closed the door.

"The bottles!" Cassidy shouted.

"A celebration!"

"By God, we deserve a celebration!"

Professor Meyer smiled—internally only, of course, since
his facial expressions were now limited.

Feldman came up to him. "How do you feel, sir?"

"I am fine," Meyer said, enunciating carefully with his
strange palate. "A little confused, perhaps—"

"But not regretful?" Feldman asked.

"I don't know yet," Meyer said. "I was against this on
principle, you know. No man is indispensable."

"You are, sir." Feldman spoke with fierce conviction. "I followed your lectures. Not that I pretend to understand one
tenth of what you were saying. Mathematical symbolism is
only a hobby with me. But those unification principles—"

"Please," Meyer said.

"No, let me speak, sir," Feldman said. "You are carrying on the great work where Einstein and the others left off. No one else can complete it! No one! You had to have a few more years, in any form science could give you. I only wish we could have found a more suitable receptacle for your intellect. A human host was unavailable, and we were forced to rule out the primates—"

"It doesn't matter," Meyer said. "It's the intellect that counts, after all. I'm still a little dizzy . . ."

"I remember your last lecture at Harvard," Feldman continued, clenching his hands together. "You were so old, sir! I could have cried—that tired, ruined body—"

"Can we give you a drink, sir?" Cassidy offered Meyer a glass.

Meyer laughed. "I'm afraid my new facial configuration is not suited for glasses. A bowl would be preferable."

"Right!" Cassidy said. "One bowl coming up! Lord, Lord . . ."

"You'll have to excuse us, sir," Feldman apologized. "The strain has been terrific. We've been in this room for over a week, and I doubt if one of us had eight hours sleep in that time. We almost lost you, sir—"

"The bowl! The flowing bowl is here!" Lupowicz called. "What'll it be, sir? Rye? Gin?"

"Just water, please," Meyer said. "Do you think I could get up?"

"If you'll take it easy . . ." Lupowicz lifted him gently from the table and set him on the floor. Meyer balanced uneasily on his four legs.

The men cheered him wildly. "Bravo!"

"I believe I may be able to do some work tomorrow," Meyer said. "Some sort of an apparatus will have to be devised to enable me to write. It shouldn't be too difficult. There will be other problems attendant upon my change. I'm not thinking too clearly as yet . . ."

"Don't try to rush things."

"Hell, no! Can't lose you now!"

"What a paper this is going to make!"

"Collaborative effort, do you think, or each from his own viewpoint and specialty?"

"Both, both. They'll never get enough of this. Goddamn it, they'll be talking about this—"

"Where is the bathroom?" Meyer asked.

The men looked at each other.

"What for?"

'Shut up, you idiot. This way, sir. I'll open the door for you."

Meyer followed at the man's heels, perceiving, as he walked, the greater ease inherent in four-legged locomotion. When he returned, the men were talking heatedly about technical aspects of his case.

"—never again in a million years."

"I can't agree with you. Anything we can do once—"

"Don't get scientific on us, kid. You know damned well it was a weird combination of fortuitous factors—plain blind luck!"

"You can say that again. Some of those bio-electric changes—"

"He's back."

"Yeah, but he shouldn't be walking around too much. How you feeling, boy?"

"I'm not a boy," Professor Meyer snapped. "I'm old enough to be your grandfather."

"Sorry, sir. I think you should go to bed, sir."

"Yes," Professor Meyer said. "I'm not too strong yet, not too clear . . ."

Kent lifted him and placed him on the cot. "There, how's that?"

They gathered around him, their arms linked around each other's shoulders. They were grinning, and very proud of themselves.

"Anything we can get you?"

"Just call for it, we'll bring it."

"Here, I've filled your bowl with water."

"We'll leave a couple sandwiches by your cot."

"Have a good rest," Cassidy said tenderly.

Then, involuntarily, absent-mindedly, he patted Professor Meyer on his long, smooth-furred head.

Feldman shouted something incoherent.

"I forgot," Cassidy said in embarrassed apology.

"We'll have to watch ourselves. He's a man, you know."

"Of course I know. I must be tired . . . I mean, he *looks* so much like a dog, you kinda forget—"

"Get out of here!" Feldman ordered. "Get out! All of you!"

He pushed them out of the room and hurried back to Professor Meyer.

"Is there anything I can do, sir? Anything at all?"

Meyer tried to speak, to reaffirm his humanity. But the words came out choked.

"It'll never happen again, sir. I'm sure of it. Why, you're—you're Professor Meyer!"

Quickly Feldman pulled a blanket over Meyer's shivering body.

"It's all right, sir," Feldman said, trying not to look at the shivering animal. "It's the intellect that counts, sir. The mind!"

"Of course," agreed Professor Meyer, the eminent mathematician. "But I wonder—would you mind patting my head for me, please?"

EARLY
MODEL

The landing was almost a catastrophe. Bentley knew his coordination was impaired by the bulky weight on his back; he didn't realize how much until, at a crucial moment, he stabbed the wrong button. The ship began to drop like a stone. At the last moment, he overcompensated, scorching a black hole into the plain below him. His ship touched, teetered for a moment, then sickeningly came to rest.

Bentley had effected mankind's first landing on Tels IV.

His immediate reaction was to pour himself a sizable drink of strictly medicinal scotch.

When that was out of the way, he turned on his radio. The receiver was imbedded in his ear, where it itched, and the microphone was a surgically implanted lump in his throat. The portable sub-space set was self-tuning, which was all to the good, since Bentley knew nothing about narrowcasting on so tight a beam over so great a distance.

"All's well," he told Professor Sliggert over the radio. "It's an Earth-type planet, just as the survey reports said. The ship is intact. And I'm happy to report that I did not break my neck in landing."

"Of course not," Sliggert said, his voice thin and emotionless through the tiny receiver. "What about the Protec? How does it feel? Have you become used to it yet."

Bentley said, "Nope. It still feels like a monkey on my back."

"Well, you'll adjust," Sliggert assured him. "The Institute sends its congratulations and I believe the government is awarding you a medal of some sort. Remember, the thing now is to fraternize with the aborigines, and if possible to establish a trade agreement of some sort, any sort. As a precedent. We need this planet, Bentley."

"I know."

"Good luck. Report whenever you have a chance."

"I'll do that," Bentley promised and signed off.

He tried to stand up, but didn't make it on the first attempt. Then, using the handholds that had been conveniently spaced above the control board, he managed to stagger erect.

Now he appreciated the toll that no-weight extracts from a man's muscles. He wished he had done his exercises more faithfully on the long trip out from Earth.

Bentley was a big, jaunty young man, over six feet tall, widely and solidly constructed. On Earth, he had weighed two hundred pounds and had moved with an athlete's grace. But ever since leaving Earth, he'd had the added encumbrance of seventy-three pounds strapped irrevocably and immovably to his back. Under the circumstances, his movements resembled those of a very old elephant wearing tight shoes.

He moved his shoulders under the wide plastic straps, grimaced, and walked to a starboard porthole. In the distance, perhaps half a mile away, he could see a village, low and brown on the horizon. There were dots on the plain moving toward him. The villagers apparently had decided to discover what strange object had fallen from the skies breathing fire and making an uncanny noise.

"Good show," Bentley said to himself. Contact would have been difficult if these aliens had shown no curiosity. This eventuality had been considered by the Earth Interstellar Exploration Institute, but no solution had been found. Therefore it had been struck from the list of possibilities.

The villagers were drawing closer. Bentley decided it was time to get ready. He opened a locker and took out his linguascene, which, with some difficulty, he strapped to his chest. On one hip, he fastened a large canteen of water. On the other hip went a package of concentrated food. Across his stomach, he put a package of assorted tools. Strapped to one leg was the radio. Strapped to the other was a medicine kit.

Thus equipped, Bentley was carrying a total of 148 pounds, every ounce of it declared essential for an extraterrestrial explorer.

The fact that he lurched rather than walked was considered unimportant.

The natives had reached the ship now and were gathering around it, commenting disparagingly. They were bipeds. They had short thick tails and their features were human, but nightmare human. Their coloring was a vivid orange.

Bentley also noticed that they were armed. He could see knives, spears, lances, stone hammers and flint axes. At the sight of this armament, a satisfied smile broke over his face. Here was the justification for his discomfort, the reason for the unwieldy seventy-three pounds which had remained on his back ever since leaving Earth.

It didn't matter what weapons these aboriginals had, right up to the nuclear level. They couldn't hurt him.

That's what Professor Sliggert, head of the Institute, inventor of the Protec, had told him.

Bentley opened the port. A cry of astonishment came from the Telians. His linguascene, after a few seconds' initial hesitation, translated the cries as, "Oh! Ah! How strange! Unbelievable! Ridiculous! Shockingly improper!"

Bentley descended the ladder on the ship's side, carefully balancing his 148 pounds of excess weight. The natives formed a semicircle around him, their weapons ready.

He advanced on them. They shrank back. Smiling pleasantly, he said, "I come as a friend." The linguascene barked out the harsh consonants of the Telian language.

They didn't seem to believe him. Spears were poised and one Telian, larger than the others and wearing a colorful headdress, held a hatchet in readiness.

Bentley felt the slightest tremor run through him. He was invulnerable, of course. There was nothing they could do to him as long as he wore the Protec. Nothing! Professor Sliggert had been certain of it.

Before takeoff, Professor Sliggert had strapped the Protec to Bentley's back, adjusted the straps and stepped back to admire his brainchild.

"Perfect," he had announced with quiet pride.

Bentley had shrugged his shoulders under the weight. "Kind of heavy, isn't it?"

"But what can we do?" Sliggert asked him. "This is the first of its kind, the prototype. I have used every weight-saving device possible—transistors, light alloys, printed circuits, pencil-power packs and all the rest. Unfortunately, early models of any invention are invariably bulky."

"Seems as though you could have streamlined it a bit," Bentley objected, peering over his shoulder.

"Streamlining comes much later. First must be concentration, then compaction, then group-function, and finally styling. It's always been that way and it will always be. Take the typewriter. Now it is simply a keyboard, almost as flat as a briefcase. But the prototype typewriter worked with foot pedals and required the combined strength of several men to lift. Take the hearing aid, which actually shrank pounds through the various stages of its development. Take the linguascene, which began as a very massive, complicated electronic calculator weighing several tons—"

"Okay," Bentley broke in. "If this is the best you could make it, good enough. How do I get out of it?"

Professor Sliggert smiled.

Bentley reached around. He couldn't find a buckle. He pulled ineffectually at the shoulder straps, but could find no way of undoing them. Nor could he squirm out. It was like being in a new and fiendishly efficient straitjacket.

"Come on, Professor, how do I get it off?"

"I'm not going to tell you."

"Huh?"

"The Protec is uncomfortable, is it not?" Sliggert asked. "You would rather not wear it?"

"You're damned right."

"Of course. Did you know that in wartime, on the battlefield, soldiers have a habit of discarding essential equipment because it is bulky or uncomfortable? But we can't take chances on you. You are going to an alien planet, Mr. Bentley. You will be exposed to wholly unknown dangers. It is necessary that you be protected at all times."

"I know that," Bentley said. "I've got enough sense to figure out when to wear this thing."

"But do you? We selected you for attributes such as resourcefulness, stamina, physical strength—and, of course, a certain amount of intelligence. But—"

"Thanks!"

"But those qualities do not make you prone to caution. Suppose you found the natives seemingly friendly and decided to discard the heavy, uncomfortable Protec? What would happen if you had misjudged their attitude? This is very easy to do on Earth; think how much easier it will be on an alien planet!"

"I can take care of myself," Bentley said.

Sliggert nodded grimly. "That is what Atwood said when he left for Durabella II and we have never heard from him again. Nor have we heard from Blake, or Smythe, or Korishell. Can you turn a knife-thrust from the rear? Have you eyes in the back of your head? No, Mr. Bentley, you haven't—but *the Protec has!*"

"Look," Bentley had said, "believe it or not, I'm a responsible adult. I will wear the Protec at all times when on the surface of an alien planet. Now tell me how to get it off."

"You don't seem to realize something, Bentley. If only your life were at stake, we would let you take what risks seemed reasonable to you. But we are also risking several billion dollars' worth of spaceship and equipment. Moreover, this is the Protec's field test. The only way to be sure of the results is to have you wear it all the time. The only way to ensure *that* is by not telling you how to remove it. We want results. You are going to stay alive whether you like it or not."

Bentley had thought it over and agreed grudgingly. "I guess I might be tempted to take it off, if the natives were really friendly."

"You will be spared that temptation. Now do you understand how it works?"

"Sure," Bentley said. "But will it really do all you say?"

"It passed the lab tests perfectly."

"I'd hate to have some little thing go wrong. Suppose it pops a fuse or blows a wire?"

"That is one of the reasons for its bulk," Sliggert explained patiently. "Triple everything. We are taking no chance of mechanical failure.

"And the power supply?"

"Good for a century or better at full load. The Protec is perfect, Bentley! After this field test, I have no doubt it will become standard equipment for all extraterrestrial explorers." Professor Sliggert permitted himself a faint smile of pride.

"All right," Bentley had said, moving his shoulders under the wide plastic straps. "I'll get used to it."

But he hadn't. A man just doesn't get used to a seventy-three-pound monkey on his back.

The Telians didn't know what to make of Bentley. They argued for several minutes, while the explorer kept a strained smile on his face. Then one Telian stepped forward. He was taller than the others and wore a distinctive headdress made of glass, bones and bits of rather garishly painted wood.

"My friends," the Telian said, "there is an evil here which I, Rinek, can sense."

Another Telian wearing a similar headdress stepped forward and said, "It is not well for a ghost doctor to speak of such things."

"Of course not," Rinek admitted. "It is not well to speak of evil in the presence of evil, for evil then grows strong. But a ghost doctor's work is the detection and avoidance of evil.

In this work, we must persevere, no matter what the risk."

Several other men in the distinctive headdress, the ghost doctors, had come forward now. Bentley decided that they were the Telian equivalent of priests and probably wielded considerable political power as well.

"I don't think he's evil," a young and cheerful-looking ghost doctor named Huascl said.

"Of course he is. Just look at him."

Appearances prove nothing, as we know from the time the good spirit Ahut M'Kandi appeared in the form of a—"

"No lectures, Huascl. All of us know the parables of Lalland. The point is, can we take a chance?"

Huascl turned to Bentley. "Are you evil?" the Telian asked earnestly.

"No," Bentley said. He had been puzzled at first by the Telians' intense preoccupation with his spiritual status. They hadn't even asked him where he'd come from, or how, or why. But then, it was not so strange. If an alien had landed on Earth during certain periods of religious zeal, the first question asked might have been, "Are you a creature of God or of Satan?"

"He says he's not evil," Huascl said.

"How would he know?"

"If he doesn't, who does?"

"Once the great spirit G'tal presented a wise man with three kdal and said to him—"

And on it went. Bentley found his legs beginning to bend under the weight of all his equipment. The linguascene was no longer able to keep pace with the shrill theological discussion that raged around him. His status seemed to depend upon two or three disputed points, none of which the ghost doctors wanted to talk about, since to talk about evil was in itself dangerous.

To make matters more complicated, there was a schism over the concept of the penetrability of evil, the younger ghost doctors holding to one side, the older to the other. The factions accused each other of rankest heresy, but Bentley couldn't figure out who believed what or which interpretation aided him.

When the sun drooped low over the grassy plain, the battle still raged. Then, suddenly, the ghost doctors reached an agreement, although Bentley couldn't decide why or on what basis.

Huascl stepped forward as spokesman for the younger ghost doctors.

"Stranger," he declared, "we have decided not to kill you."

Bentley suppressed a smile. That was just like a primitive people, granting life to an invulnerable being!

"Not yet, anyhow," Huascl amended quickly, catching a frown upon Rinek and the older ghost doctors. "It depends entirely upon you. We will go to the village and purify ourselves and we will feast. Then we will initiate you into the society of ghost doctors. No evil thing can become a ghost doctor; it is expressly forbidden. In this manner, we will detect your true nature."

"I am deeply grateful," Bentley said.

"But if you are evil, we are pledged to destroy evil. And if we must, we can!"

The assembled Telians cheered his speech and began at once the mile trek to the village. Now that a status had been assigned Bentley, even tentatively, the natives were completely friendly. They chatted amiably with him about crops, droughts and famines.

Bentley staggered along under his equipment, tired, but inwardly elated. This was really a coup! As an initiate, a priest, he would have an unsurpassed opportunity to gather anthropological data, to establish trade, to pave the way for the future development of Tels IV.

All he had to do was pass the initiation tests. And not get killed, of course, he reminded himself, smiling.

It was funny how positive the ghost doctors had been that they could kill him.

The village consisted of two dozen huts arranged in a rough circle. Beside each mud-and-thatch hut was a small vegetable garden, and sometimes a pen for the Telian version of cattle. There were small green-furred animals roaming between the huts, which the Telians treated as pets. The grassy central area was common ground. Here was the community well and here were the shrines to various gods and devils. In this area, lighted by a great bonfire, a feast had been laid out by the village women.

Bentley arrived at the feast in a state of near-exhaustion, stooped beneath his essential equipment. Gratefully, he sank to the ground with the villagers and the celebration began.

First the village women danced a welcoming for him. They made a pretty sight, their orange skin glinting in the firelight, their tails swinging gracefully in unison. Then a village dignitary named Occip came over to him, bearing a full bowl.

"Stranger," Occip said, "you are from a distant land and your ways are not our ways. Yet let us be brothers! Partake, therefore, of this food to seal the bond between us, and in the name of all sanctity!"

Bowing low, he offered the bowl.

It was an important moment, one of those pivotal occasions that can seal forever the friendship between races or make them eternal enemies. But Bentley was not able to take advantage of it. As tactfully as he could, he refused the symbolic food.

"But it is purified!" Occip said.

Bentley explained that, because of a tribal taboo, he could eat only his own food. Occip could not understand that different species have different dietary requirements. For example, Bentley pointed out, the staff of life on Tels IV might well be some strychnine compound. But he did not add that even if he wanted to take the chance, his Protec would never allow it.

Nonetheless, his refusal alarmed the village. There were hurried conferences among the ghost doctors. Then Rinek came over and sat beside him.

"Tell me," Rinek inquired after a while, "what do you think of evil?"

"Evil is not good," Bentley said solemnly.

"Ah!" The ghost doctor pondered that, his tail flicking nervously over the grass. A small green-furred pet, a mog, began to play with his tail. Rinek pushed him away and said, "So you do not like evil."

"No."

"And you would permit no evil influence around you?"

"Certainly not," Bentley said, stifling a yawn. He was growing bored with the ghost doctor's tortuous examining.

"In that case, you would have no objection to receiving the sacred and very holy spear that Kran K'leu brought down from the abode of the Small Gods, the brandishing of which confers good upon a man."

"I would be pleased to receive it," said Bentley, heavy-eyed, hoping this would be the last ceremony of the evening.

Rinek grunted his approval and moved away. The women's dances came to an end. The ghost doctors began to chant in deep, impressive voices. The bonfire flared high.

Huascl came forward. His face was now painted in thin

black and white stripes. He carried an ancient spear of black wood, its head of shaped volcanic glass, its length intricately although primitively carved.

Holding the spear aloft, Huascl said. "O Stranger from the Skies, accept from us this spear of sanctity! Kran K'leu gave this lance to Trin, our first father, and bestowed upon it a magical nature and caused it to be a vessel of the spirits of the good. Evil cannot abide the presence of this spear! Take, then, our blessings with it."

Bentley heaved himself to his feet. He understood the value of a ceremony like this. His acceptance of the spear should end, once and for all, any doubts as to his spiritual status. Reverently he inclined his head.

Huascl came forward, held out the spear and—

The Protec snapped into action.

Its operation was simple, in common with many great inventions. When its calculator-component received a danger cue, the Protec threw a force field around its operator. This field rendered him invulnerable, for it was completely and absolutely impenetrable. But there were certain unavoidable disadvantages.

If Bentley had had a weak heart, the Protec might have killed him there and then, for its action was electronically sudden, completely unexpected and physically wrenching. One moment, he was standing in front of the great bonfire, his hand held out for the sacred spear. In the next moment, he was plunged into darkness.

As usual, he felt as though he had been catapulted into a musty, lightless closet, with rubbery walls pressing close on all sides. He cursed the machine's super-efficiency. The spear had not been a threat; it was part of an important ceremony. But the Protec, with its literal senses, had interpreted it as a possible danger.

Now, in the darkness, Bentley fumbled for the controls that would release the field. As usual, the force field interfered with his positional sense, a condition that seemed to grow worse with each subsequent use. Carefully he felt his way along his chest, where the button should have been, and located it at last under his right armpit, where it had twisted around to. He released the field.

The feast had ended abruptly. The natives were standing close together for protection, weapons ready, tails stretched stiffly out. Huascl, caught in the force field's range, had been flung twenty feet and was slowly picking himself up.

The ghost doctors began to chant a purification dirge, for protection against evil spirits. Bentley couldn't blame them.

When a Protec force field goes on, it appears as an opaque black sphere, some ten feet in diameter. If it is struck, it repels with a force equal to the impact. White lines appear in the sphere's surface, swirl, coalesce, vanish. And as the sphere spins, it screams in a thin, high-pitched wail.

All in all, it was a sight hardly calculated to win the confidence of a primitive and superstitious people.

"Sorry," Bentley said, with a weak smile. There hardly seemed anything else to say.

Huascl limped back, but kept his distance. "You cannot accept the sacred spear," he stated.

"Well, it's not exactly that," said Bentley. "It's just—well, I've got this protective device, kind of like a shield, you know? It doesn't like spears. Couldn't you offer me a sacred gourd?"

"Don't be ridiculous," Huascl said. "Who ever heard of a sacred gourd?"

"No, I guess not. But please take my word for it—I'm not evil. Really I'm not. I've just got a taboo about spears."

The ghost doctors talked among themselves too rapidly for the linguascene to interpret it. It caught only the words "evil," "destroy," and "purification." Bentley decided his forecast didn't look too favorable.

After the conference, Huascl came over to him and said, "Some of the others feel that you should be killed at once, before you bring some great unhappiness upon the village. I told them, however, that you cannot be blamed for the many taboos that restrict you. We will pray for you through the night. And perhaps, in the morning, the initiation will be possible."

Bentley thanked him. He was shown to a hut and then the Telians left him as quickly as possible. There was an ominous hush over the village; from his doorway, Bentley could see little groups of natives talking earnestly and glancing covertly in his direction.

It was a poor beginning for cooperation between two races.

He immediately contacted Professor Sliggert and told him what had happened.

"Unfortunate," the professor said. "But primitive people are notoriously treacherous. They might have meant to kill you with the spear instead of actually handing it to you. Let you have it, that is, in the most literal sense."

"I'm positive there was no such intention," Bentley said. "After all, you have to start trusting people sometime."

"Not with a billion dollars' worth of equipment in your charge."

"But I'm not going to be able to *do* anything!" Bentley shouted. "Don't you understand? They're suspicious of me already. I wasn't able to accept their sacred spear. That means I'm very possibly evil. Now what if I can't pass the initiation ceremony tomorrow? Suppose some idiot starts to pick his teeth with a knife and the Protec saves me? All the favorable first impression I built up will be lost."

"Good will can be regained," Professor Sliggert said sententiously. "But a billion dollars' worth of equipment—"

"—can be salvaged by the next expedition. Look, Professor, give me a break. Isn't there some way I can control this thing manually?"

"No way at all," Sliggert replied. "That would defeat the entire purpose of the machine. You might just as well not be wearing it if you're allowed to rely on your own reflexes rather than electronic impulses."

"Then tell me how to take it off."

"The same argument holds true—you wouldn't be protected at all times."

"Look," Bentley protested, "you chose me as a competent explorer. I'm the guy on the spot. I know what the conditions are here. Tell me how to get it off."

"No! The Protec must have a full field test. And we want you to come back alive."

"That's another thing," Bentley said. "These people seem kind of sure they can kill me."

"Primitive peoples always overestimate the potency of their strength, weapons and magic."

"I know, I know. But you're certain there's no way they can get through the field? Poison, maybe?"

"Nothing can get through the field," Sliggert said patiently. "Not even light rays can penetrate. Not even gamma radiation. You are wearing an impregnable fortress, Mr. Bentley. Why can't you manage to have a little faith in it?"

"Early models of inventions sometimes need a lot of ironing out," Bentley grumbled. "But have it your way.

Won't you tell me how to take it off, though, just in case something goes wrong?"

"I wish you would stop asking me that, Mr. Bentley. You were chosen to give Protec a *full* field test. That's just what you are going to do."

When Bentley signed off, it was deep twilight outside and the villagers had returned to their huts. Campfires burned low and he could hear the call of night creatures.

At that moment, Bentley felt very alien and exceedingly homesick.

He was tired almost to the point of unconsciousness, but he forced himself to eat some concentrated food and drink a little water. Then he unstrapped the tool kit, the radio and the canteen, tugged defeatedly at the Protec, and lay down to sleep.

Just as he dozed off, the Protec went violently into action, nearly snapping his neck out of joint.

Wearily he fumbled for the controls, located them near his stomach, and turned off the field.

The hut looked exactly the same. He could find no source of attack.

Was the Protec losing its grip on reality, he wondered, or had a Telian tried to spear him through the window?

Then Bentley saw a tiny mog puppy scuttling away frantically, its legs churning up clouds of dust.

The little beast probably just wanted to get warm, Bentley thought. But of course it was alien. Its potential for danger could not be overlooked by the ever-wary Protec.

He fell asleep again and immediately began to dream that he was locked in a prison of bright red sponge rubber. He could push the walls out and out and out, but they never yielded, and at last he would have to let go and be gently shoved back to the center of the prison. Over and over, this happened, until suddenly he felt his back wrenched and awoke within the Protec's lightless field.

This time he had real difficulty finding the controls. He hunted desperately by feel until the bad air made him gasp in panic. He located the controls at last under his chin, released the field, and began to search groggily for the source of the new attack.

He found it. A twig had fallen from the thatch roof and had tried to land on him. The Protec, of course, had not allowed it.

"Aw, come on now," Bentley groaned aloud. "Let's use a little judgment!"

But he was really too tired to care. Fortunately, there were no more assaults that night.

Huascl came to Bentley's hut in the morning, looking very solemn and considerably disturbed.

"There were great sounds from your hut during the night," the ghost doctor said, "Sounds of torment, as though you were wrestling with a devil."

"I'm just a restless sleeper," Bentley explained.

Huascl smiled to show that he appreciated the joke. "My friend, did you pray for purification last night and for release from evil?"

"I certainly did."

"And was your prayer granted?"

"It was," Bentley said hopefully. "There's no evil around me. Not a a bit."

Huascl looked dubious. "But can you be sure? Perhaps you should depart from us in peace. If you cannot be initiated, we shall have to destroy you—"

"Don't worry about it," Bentley told him. "Let's get started."

"Very well," Huascl said, and together they left the hut.

The initiation was to be held in front of the great bonfire in the village square. Messengers had been sent out during the night and ghost doctors from many villages were there. Some had come as far as twenty miles to take part in the rites and to see the alien with their own eyes. The ceremonial drum had been taken from its secret hiding place and was now booming solemnly. The villagers watched, chattered together, laughed. But Bentley could detect an undercurrent of nervousness and strain.

There was a long series of dances. Bentley twitched worriedly when the last figure started, for the leading dancer was swinging a glass-studded club around his head. Nearer and nearer the dancer whirled, now only a few feet away from him, his club a dazzling streak.

The villagers watched, fascinated. Bentley shut his eyes, expecting to be plunged momentarily into the darkness of the force field.

But the dancer moved away at last and the dance ended with a roar of approval from the villagers.

Huascl began to speak. Bentley realized with a thrill of relief that this was the end of the ceremony.

"O brothers," Huascl said, "this alien has come across the great emptiness to be our brother. Many of his ways are strange and around him there seems to hang a strange hint of evil. And yet who can doubt that he means well? Who can doubt that he is, in essence, a good and honorable person? With this initiation, we purge him of evil and make him one of us."

There was dead silence as Huascl walked up to Bentley. "Now," Huascl said, "you are a ghost doctor and indeed one of us." He held out his hand.

Bentley felt his heart leap within him. He had won! He had been accepted! He reached out and clasped Huascl's hand.

Or tried to. He didn't quite make it, for the Protec, ever alert, saved him from the possibly dangerous contact.

"You damned idiotic gadget!" Bentley bellowed, quickly finding the control and releasing the field.

He saw at once that the fat was in the fire.

"Evil!" shrieked the Telians, frenziedly waving their weapons.

"Evil!" screamed the ghost doctors.

Bentley turned despairingly to Huascl.

"Yes," the young ghost doctor said sadly, "it is true. We had hoped to cure the evil by our ancient ceremonial. But it could not be. This evil must be destroyed! *Kill the devil!*"

A shower of spears came at Bentley. The Protec responded instantly.

Soon it was apparent that an impasse had been reached. Bentley would remain for a few minutes in the field, then override the controls. The Telians, seeing him still unharmed, would renew their barrage and the Protec would instantly go back into action.

Bentley tried to walk back to his ship. But the Protec went on again each time he shut it off. It would take him a month or two to cover a mile, at that rate, so he stopped trying. He would simply wait the attackers out. After a while, they would find out they couldn't hurt him and the two races would finally get down to business.

He tried to relax within the field, but found it impossible. He was hungry and extremely thirsty. And his air was starting to grow stale.

Then Bentley remembered, with a sense of shock, that air had not gone through the surrounding field the night before. Naturally—nothing could get through. If he wasn't careful, he could be asphyxiated.

Even an impregnable fortress could fall, he knew, if the defenders were starved or suffocated out.

He began to think furiously. How long could the Telians keep up the attack? They would have to grow tired sooner or later, wouldn't they?

Or would they?

He waited as long as he could, until the air was all but unbreathable, then overrode the controls. The Telians were sitting on the ground around him. Fires had been lighted and food was cooking. Rinek lazily threw a spear at him and the field went on.

So, Bentley thought, they had learned. They were going to starve him out.

He tried to think, but the walls of his dark closet seemed to be pressing against him. He was growing claustrophobic and already his air was stale again.

He thought for a moment, then overrode the controls. The Telians looked at him coolly. One of them reached for a spear.

"Wait!" Bentley shouted. At the same moment, he turned on his radio.

"What do you want?" Rinek asked.

"Listen to me! It isn't fair to trap me in the Protec like this!"

"Eh? What's going on?" Professor Sliggert asked, through the ear receiver.

"You Telians know—" Bentley said hoarsely—"you know that you can destroy me by continually activating the Protec. I can't turn it off! I can't get out of it!"

"Ah!" said Professor Sliggert. "I see the difficulty. Yes."

"We are sorry," Huascl apologized. "But evil must be destroyed."

"Of course it must," Bentley said desperately. "But not me. Give me a chance. *Professor!*"

"This is indeed a flaw," Professor Sliggert mused, "and a serious one. Strange, but things like this, of course, can't show up in the lab, only in a full-scale field test. The fault will be rectified in the new models."

"Great! But I'm here now! How do I get this thing off?"

"I am sorry," Sliggert said. "I honestly never thought the need would arise. To tell the truth, I designed the harness so that you could not get out of it under any circumstances."

"Why, you lousy—"

"Please!" Sliggert said sternly. "Let's keep our heads. If you can hold out for a few months, we might be able—"

"I can't! The air! Water!"

"Fire!" cried Rinek, his face contorted. "By fire, we will chain the demon!"

And the Protec snapped on.

Bentley tried to think things out carefully in the darkness. He would have to get out of the Protec. But how? There was a knife in his tool kit. Could he cut through the tough plastic straps? He would have to!

But what then? Even if he emerged from his fortress, the ship was a mile away. Without the Protec, they could kill him with a single spear thrust. And they were pledged to, for he had been declared irrevocably evil.

But if he ran, he at least had a chance. And it was better to die of a spear thrust than to strangle slowly in absolute darkness.

Bentley turned off the field. The Telians were surrounding him with campfires, closing off his retreat with a wall of flame.

He hacked frantically at the plastic web. The knife slithered and slipped along the strap. And he was back in Protec.

When he came out again, the circle of fire was complete. The Telians were cautiously pushing the fires toward him, lessening the circumference of his circle.

Bentley felt his heart sink. Once the fires were close enough, the Protec would go on and stay on. He would not be able to override a continuous danger signal. He would be trapped within the field for as long as they fed the flames.

And considering how primitive people felt about devils, it was just possible that they would keep the fire going for a century or two.

He dropped the knife, used side-cutters on the plastic strap and succeeded in ripping it halfway through.

He was in Protec again.

Bentley was dizzy, half-fainting from fatigue, gasping great mouthfuls of foul air. With an effort, he pulled himself together. He couldn't drop now. That would be the end.

He found the controls, overrode them. The fires were very near him now. He could feel their warmth against his face. He snipped viciously at the strap and felt it give.

He slipped out of the Protec just as the field activated again. The force of it threw him into the fire. But he fell feet-first and jumped out of the flames without getting burned.

The villagers roared. Bentley sprinted away; as he ran, he dumped the linguascene, the tool kit, the radio, the concentrated food and the canteen. He glanced back once and saw that the Telians were after him.

But he was holding his own. His tortured heart seemed to be pounding his chest apart and his lungs threatened to collapse at any moment. But now the spaceship was before him, looming great and friendly on the flat plain.

He was going to just make it. Another twenty yards . . .

Something green flashed in front of him. It was a small, green-furred mog puggy. The clumsy beast was trying to get out of his way.

He swerved to avoid crushing it and realized too late that he should never have broken stride. A rock turned under his foot and he sprawled forward.

He heard the pounding feet of the Telians coming toward him and manged to climb on one knee.

Then somebody threw a club and it landed neatly on his forehead.

"Ar gwy dril?" a voice asked incomprehensibly from far off.

Bentley opened his eyes and saw Huascl bending over him. He was in a hut, back in the village. Several armed ghost doctors were at the doorway, watching.

"Ar dril?" Huascl asked again.

Bentley rolled over and saw, piled neatly beside him, his canteen, concentrated food, tools, radio and linguascene. He took a deep drink of water, then turned on the linguascene.

"I asked if you felt all right," Huascl said.

"Sure, fine," Bentley grunted, feeling his head. "Let's get it over with."

"Over with?"

"You're going to kill me, aren't you? Well, let's not make a production out of it."

"But we didn't want to destroy you," Huascl said. "We knew you for a good man. It was the devil we wanted!"

"Eh?" asked Bentley in a blank uncomprehending voice.

"Come, look."

The ghost doctors helped Bentley to his feet and brought

him outside. There, surrounded by lapping flames, was the glowing great black sphere of the Protec.

"You didn't know, of course," Huascl said, "but there was a devil riding upon your back."

"Huh!" gasped Bentley.

"Yes, it is true. We tried to dispossess him by purification, but he was too strong. We had to force you, brother, to face that evil and throw it aside. We knew you would come through. And you did!"

"I see," Bentley said. "A devil on my back. Yes, I guess so."

That was exactly what the Protec would have to be, to them. A heavy, misshapen weight on his shoulders, hurling out a black sphere whenever they tried to purify it. What else could a religious people do but try to free him from its grasp?

He saw several women of the village bring up baskets of food and throw them into the fire in front of the sphere. He looked inquiringly at Huascl.

"We are propitiating it," Huascl said, "for it is a very strong devil, undoubtedly a miracle-working one. Our village is proud to have such a devil in bondage."

A ghost doctor from a neighboring village stepped up. "Are there more such devils in your homeland? Could you bring us one to worship?"

Several other ghost doctors pressed eagerly forward. Bently nodded. "It can be arranged," he said.

He knew that the Earth-Tels trade was now begun. And at last a suitable use had been found for Professor Sliggert's Protec.

DISPOSAL
SERVICE

The visitor shouldn't have gotten past the reception desk, for Mr. Ferguson saw people by appointment only, unless they were very important. His time was worth money, and he had to protect it.

But his secretary, Miss Dale, was young and easily impressed; and the visitor was old, and he wore conservative English tweeds, carried a cane, and held an engraved business card. Miss Dale thought he was important, and ushered him directly into Mr. Ferguson's office.

"Good morning, sir," the visitor said as soon as Miss Dale had closed the door. "I am Mr. Esmond from the Disposal Service." He handed Ferguson his card.

"I see," Ferguson said, annoyed at Miss Dale's lack of judgment. "Disposal Service? Sorry, I have nothing I wish disposed of." He rose, to cut the interview short.

"Nothing whatsoever?" Mr. Esmond asked.

"Not a thing. Thank you for calling—"

"I take it, then, that you are content with the people around you?"

"What? How's that any of your business?"

"Why, Mr. Ferguson, that is the function of the Disposal Service."

"You're kidding me," Ferguson said.

"Not at all," Mr. Esmond said, with some surprise.

"You mean," Ferguson said, laughing, "you dispose of people?"

"Of course. I cannot produce any personal endorsements, for we are at some pains to avoid all advertising. But I can assure you we are an old and reliable firm."

Ferguson stared at the neat, stiffly erect Esmond. He didn't know how to take this. It was a joke, of course. Anyone could see that.

It had to be a joke.

"And what do you do with the people you dispose of?" Ferguson asked jovially.

"That," Mr. Esmond said, "is our concern. To all intents and purposes, they disappear."

Ferguson stood up. "All right, Mr. Esmond. What really is your business?"

"I've told you," Esmond said.

"Come now. You weren't serious. . . . If I thought you were serious, I'd call the police."

Mr. Esmond sighed and stood up. "I take it, then, you have no need of our services. You are entirely satisfied with your friends, relatives, wife."

"My wife? What do you know about my wife?"

"Nothing, Mr. Ferguson."

"Have you been talking to our neighbors? Those quarrels mean nothing, absolutely nothing."

"I have no information about your marital state, Mr. Ferguson," Esmond said, sitting down again.

"Then why did you ask about my wife?"

"We have found that marriages are our chief source of revenue."

"Well, there's nothing wrong with my marriage. My wife and I get along very well."

"Then you don't need the Disposal Service," Mr. Esmond said, tucking his cane under his arm.

"Just a moment." Ferguson began to pace the floor, hands clasped behind his back. "I don't believe a word of this, you understand. Not a word. But assuming, for a moment, that you were serious. Merely assuming, mind you— what would the procedure be if I—if I wanted—"

"Just your verbal consent," Mr. Esmond said.

"Payment?"

"After disposal, not before."

"Not that I care," Ferguson said hastily. "I'm just curious." He hesitated. "Is it painful?"

"Not in the slightest."

Ferguson continued to pace. "My wife and I get along very well," he said. "We have been married for seventeen years. Of course, people always have difficulty living together. It's to be expected."

Mr. Esmond's face was expressionless.

"One learns to compromise," Ferguson said. "And I have passed the age when a passing fancy would cause me to— to—"

"I quite understand," Mr. Esmond said.

"I mean to say," Ferguson said, "my wife can, of course, be difficult. Vituperative. Nagging. I suppose you have information on that?"

"None," Mr. Esmond said.

"You must have! You must have had a particular reason for looking me up!"

Mr. Esmond shrugged his shoulders.

"Anyhow," Ferguson said heavily, "I'm past the age when a new arrangement is desirable. Suppose I had no wife? Suppose I could establish a liaison with, say, Miss Dale. It would be pleasant, I suppose."

"Merely pleasant," Mr. Esmond said.

"Yes. It would have no lasting value. It would lack the firm moral underpinning upon which any successful enterprise must be based."

"It would be merely pleasant," Mr. Esmond said.

"That's right. Enjoyable, of course. Miss Dale is an attractive woman. No one would deny that. She has an even temper, an agreeable nature, a desire to please. I'll grant all that."

Mr. Esmond smiled politely, stood up and started to the door.

"Could I let you know?" Ferguson asked suddenly.

"You have my card. I can be reached at that number until five o'clock. But you must decide by then. Time is money, and our schedule must be kept up."

"Of course," Ferguson said. He laughed hollowly. "I still don't believe a word of this. I don't even know your terms."

"Moderate, I assure you, for a man in your circumstances."

"And I would disclaim all knowledge of ever having met you, talked with you, anything."

"Naturally."

"And you *will* be at this number?"

"Until five o'clock. Good day, Mr. Ferguson."

After Esmond left, Ferguson found that his hands were shaking. The talk had disturbed him, and he determined to put it out of mind at once.

But it wasn't that easy. Although he bent earnestly over his papers, forcing his pen to make notes, he was remembering everything Esmond had said.

The Disposal Service had found out, somehow, about his wife's shortcomings. Esmond had said she was argumentative, vituperative, nagging. He was forced to recognize those truths, unpalatable though they might be. It took a stranger to look at things with a clear, unprejudiced eye.

He returned to his work. But Miss Dale came in with the morning mail, and Mr. Ferguson was forced to agree that she was extremely attractive.

"Will there be anything else, Mr. Ferguson?" she asked.

"What? Oh, not at the moment," Ferguson said. He stared at the door for a long time after she left.

Further work was impossible. He decided to go home at once.

"Miss Dale," he said, slipping on his topcoat, "I'm called away. I'm afraid a lot of work is piling up. Would it be possible for you to work with me an evening or two this week?"

"Of course, Mr. Ferguson," she said.

"I won't be interfering with your social life?" Ferguson asked, trying to laugh.

"Not at all, sir."

"I'll—I'll try to make it up to you. Business. Good day." He hurried out of the office, his cheeks burning.

At home, his wife was just finishing the wash. Mrs. Ferguson was a small, plain woman with little nervous lines around her eyes. She was surprised to see him.

"You're home early." She said.

"Is there anything wrong with that?" Ferguson asked, with an energy that surprised him.

"Of course not—"

"What do you want? Should I kill myself in that office?" he snapped.

"When did I say—"

"Kindly don't argue with me," Ferguson said. "Don't nag."

"I wasn't nagging!" his wife shouted.

"I'm going to lie down," Ferguson said.

He went upstairs and stood in front of the telephone. There was no doubt of it, everything Esmond had said was true.

He glanced at his watch, and was surprised to find that it was a quarter to five.

Ferguson began to pace in front of the telephone. He stared at Esmond's card, and a vision of the trim, attractive Miss Dale floated through his mind.

He lunged at the telephone.

"Disposal Service, Mr. Esmond speaking."

"This is Mr. Ferguson."

"Yes, sir. What have you decided?"

"I've decided . . ." Ferguson clenched the telephone tightly. He had a perfect right to do this, he told himself.

And yet, they had been married for 17 years. Seventeen years! There had been good times, as well as bad. Was it fair, was it really fair?

"What have you decided, Mr. Ferguson?" Esmond repeated.

"I—I—no! I don't want the service!" Ferguson shouted.

"Are you certain, Mr. Ferguson?"

"Yes, absolutely. You should be behind bars! Good day, sir!"

He hung up, and immediately felt an enormous weight leave his mind. He hurried downstairs.

His wife was cooking short ribs of beef, a dish he had never liked. But it didn't matter. He was prepared to overlook petty annoyances.

The doorbell rang.

"Oh, it must be the laundry," Mrs. Ferguson said, trying simultaneously to toss a salad and stir the soup. "Would you mind?"

"Not at all." Glowing in his new-found self-righteousness, Ferguson opened the door. Two uniformed men were standing outside, carrying a large canvas bag.

"Laundry?" Ferguson asked.

"Disposal Service," one of the men said.

"But I told you I didn't—"

The two men seized him, and, with the dexterity of long practice, stuffed him into the bag.

"You can't do this!" Ferguson shrieked.

The bag closed over him, and he felt himself carried down his walk. A car door creaked open, and he was laid carefully on the floor.

"Is everything all right?" he heard his wife ask.

"Yes, madam. There was a change in the schedule. We are able to fit you in after all."

"I'm so glad," he heard her say. "It was such a pleasure talking to your Mr. French this afternoon. Now excuse me. Dinner is almost ready, and I must make a phone call."

The car began to move. Ferguson tried to scream, but the canvas pressed tightly against his face.

He asked himself desperately, who could she be calling? Why didn't I suspect?

HUMAN MAN'S
BURDEN

Edward Flaswell bought his planetoid, sight unseen, at the Interstellar Land Office on Earth. He selected it on the basis of a photograph, which showed little more than a range of picturesque mountains. But Flaswell loved mountains and as he remarked to the Claims Clerk, "Might be gold in them thar hills, mightn't thar, pardner?"

"Sure, pal, sure," the clerk responded, wondering what man in his right mind would put himself several light-years from the nearest woman of any description whatsoever. No man in his right mind would, the clerk decided, and gave Flaswell a searching look.

But Flaswell was perfectly sane. He just hadn't stopped to consider the problem.

Accordingly, Flaswell put down a small sum in credits and made a large promise to improve his land every year. As soon as the ink was dry upon his deed, he purchased passage aboard a second-class drone freighter, loaded it with an assortment of secondhand equipment and set out for his holdings.

Most novice pioneers find they have purchased a sizable chunk of naked rock. Flaswell was lucky. His planetoid, which he named Chance, had a minimal manufactured atmosphere that he could boost to breathable status. There was water, which his well-digging equipment tapped on the twenty-third attempt. He found no gold in them thar hills, but there was some exportable thorium. And best of all, much of the soil was suitable for the cultivation of dir, olge, smis and other luxury fruits.

As Flaswell kept telling his robot foreman, "This place is going to make me rich!"

"Sure, Boss, sure," the robot always responded.

The planetoid had undeniable promise. Its development was an enormous task for one man, but Flaswell was only twenty-seven years old, strongly built and of a determined frame of mind. Beneath his hand, the planetoid flourished. Months passed and Flaswell planted his fields, mined his picturesque mountains and shipped his goods out by the infrequent drone freighter that passed his way.

One day, his robot foreman said to him, "Boss Man, sir, you don't look too good, Mr. Flaswell, sir."

Flaswell frowned at this speech. The man he had bought his robots from had been a Human Supremicist of the most rabid sort, who had coded the robots' responses according to his own ideas of the respect due Human People. Flaswell found this annoying, but he couldn't afford new response tapes. And where else could he have picked up robots for so little money?

"Nothing wrong with me, Gunga-Sam," Flaswell replied.

"Ah! I beg pardon! But this is not so, Mr. Flaswell, Boss. You have been talking to yourself in the fields, you should excuse my saying it."

"Aw, it's nothing."

"And you have the beginning of a tic in your left eye, sahib. And your fingers are trembling. And you are drinking too much. And—"

"That's enough, Gunga-Sam. A robot should know his place," Flaswell said. He saw the hurt expression that the robot's metal face somehow managed to convey. He sighed and said, "You're right, of course. You're always right, old friend. What's the matter with me?"

"You are bearing too much of the Human Man's Burden."

"Don't I know it!" Flaswell ran a hand through his unruly black hair. "Sometimes I envy you robots. Always laughing, carefree, happy—"

"It is because we have no souls."

"Unfortunately I do. What do you suggest?"

"Take a vacation, Mr. Flaswell, Boss," Gunga-Sam suggested, and wisely withdrew to let his master think.

Flaswell appreciated his servitor's kindly suggestion, but a vacation was difficult. His planetoid, Chance, was in the Throcian System, which was about as isolated as one could get in this day and age. True, he was only a fifteen-day flight from the tawdry amusements of Cythera III and not much farther from Nagóndicon, where considerable fun could be obtained for the strong in stomach. But distance is money, and money was the very thing Flaswell was trying to make on Chance.

He planted more crops, dug more thorium and began to grow a beard. He continued to mumble to himself in the fields and to drink heavily in the evenings. Some of the simple farm robots grew alarmed when Flaswell lurched past and they began praying to the outlawed Combustion God. But loyal Gunga-Sam soon put a stop to this ominous turn of events.

"Ignorant mechanicals!" he told them. "The Boss Human, he all right. Him strong, him good! Believe me, brothers, it is even as I say!"

But the murmurings did not cease, for robots look to Humans to set an example. The situation might have gotten out of hand if Flaswell had not received, along with his next shipment of food, a shiny new Roebuck-Ward catalogue.

Lovingly he spread it open upon his crude plastic table and, by the glow of a simple cold-light bulb, began to pore over its contents. What wonders there were for the isolated pioneer! Home distilling plants, and moon makers, and portable solidovision, and—

Flaswell turned a page, read it, gulped and read it again. It said:

MAIL ORDER BRIDES!

Pioneers, why suffer the curse of loneliness alone? Why bear the Hu-Man's Burden singly? Roebuck-Ward is now offering, for the first time, a limited selection of *Brides for the Frontiersman!*

The Roebuck-Ward Frontier Model Bride is carefully selected for strength, adaptability, agility, perseverance, pioneer skills and, of course, a measure of comeliness. These girls are conditioned to any planet, since they possess a relatively low center of gravity, a skin properly pigmented for all climates, and short, strong toe and fingernails. Shapewise, they are well proportioned and yet not distractingly contoured, a quality which the hard-working pioneer should appreciate.

The Roebuck-Ward Frontier Model comes in three general sizes (see specifications below) to suit any man's taste. Upon receipt of your request, Roebuck-Ward will quick-freeze one and ship her to you by third-class Drone Freight. In this way, your express charges are kept to an absolute minimum.

Why not order a Frontier Model Bride *TODAY?*

Flaswell called for Gunga-Sam and showed him the advertisement. Silently the mechanical read, then looked his master full in the face.

"This is surely it, effendi," the foreman said.

"You think so, huh?" Flaswell stood up and began to pace

nervously around the room. "But I wasn't planning on getting married just yet. I mean what kind of a way is this to get married? How do I know I'll like her?"

"It is proper for Human Man to have Human Woman."

"Yeah, but—"

"Besides, do they quick-freeze a preacher and ship *him* out, too?"

A slow smile broke over Flaswell's face as he digested his servant's shrewd question. "Gunga-Sam," he said, "as usual, you have gone directly to the heart of the matter. I guess there's a sort of moratorium on the ceremony while a man makes up his mind. Too expensive to quick-freeze a preacher. And it would be nice to have a gal around who could work her share."

Gunga-Sam managed to convey an inscrutable smile.

Flaswell sat down and ordered a Frontier Model Bride, specifying the small size, which he felt was plenty big enough. He gave Gunga-Sam the order to radio.

The next few weeks were filled with excitement for Flaswell and he began to scan the skies anxiously. The robots picked up the mood of anticipation. In the evenings, their carefree songs and dances were interspersed with whispering and secret merriment. The mechanicals said to Gunga-Sam over and over again, "Hey, Foreman! The new Human Woman Boss, what will she be like?"

"It's none of your concern," Gunga-Sam told them. "That's Human Man business and you robots leave it alone." But at the end, he was watching the skies as anxiously as anyone.

During those weeks, Flaswell meditated on the virtues of Frontier Woman. The more he thought about it, the more he liked the idea. No pretty, useless, helpless painted woman for him! How pleasant it would be to have a cheerful, common-sense, down-to-gravity gal who could cook, wash, pretty up the place, boss the house robots, make clothes, put up jellies. . . .

So he dreamed away the time and bit his nails to the quick.

At last the drone freighter flashed across the horizon, landed, jettisoned a large packing case, and fled in the direction of Amyra IV.

The robots brought the case to Flaswell.

"Your new bride, sir!" they shouted triumphantly, and flung their oilcans in the air.

Flaswell immediately proclaimed a half-day holiday and soon he was alone in his living room with the great frigid box marked "*Handle with Care. Woman Inside.*"

He pressed the defrosting controls, waited the requisite hour, and opened the box. Within was another box, which required two hours to defrost. Impatiently he waited, pacing up and down the room and gnawing on the remnants of his fingernails.

And then the time was up, and with shaking hands, Flaswell opened the lid and saw—

"Hey, what is this?" he cried.

The girl within the box blinked, yawned like a kitten, opened her eyes, sat up. They stared at each other and Flaswell knew that something was terribly wrong.

She was clothed in a beautiful, impractical white dress and her name, *Sheila*, was worked upon it in gold thread. The next thing Flaswell noticed was her slenderness, which was scarcely suitable for hard work on outplanet conditions. Her skin was a creamy white, obviously the kind that would blister under his planetoid's fierce summer sun. Her hands were long-fingered, red-nailed, elegant—completely unlike anything the Roebuck-Ward Company had promised. As for her legs and other parts, Flaswell decided they would be very well on Earth, but not here, where a man must pay attention to his work.

She couldn't even be said to have a low center of gravity. Quite the contrary.

Flaswell felt, not unreasonably, that he had been swindled, duped, made a fool of.

Sheila stepped out of the crate, walked to a window and looked out over Flaswell's flowering green fields and his picturesque mountains beyond them.

"But where are the palm trees?" she asked.

"Palm trees?"

"Of course. They told me that Srinigar V had palm trees."

"This is not Srinigar V," Flaswell said.

"But aren't you the Pasha of Srae?" Sheila gasped.

"Certainly not. I am a Frontiersman. Aren't you a Frontier Model Bride?"

"Do I *look* like a Frontier Model Bride?" Sheila snapped, her eyes flashing. "I am the Ultra Deluxe Luxury Model Bride and I was supposed to go to the subtropical paradise planet of Srinigar V."

"We've both been cheated. The shipping department must have made an error," Flaswell said gloomily.

The girl looked around Flaswell's crude living room and a wince twinged her pretty features. "Oh, well. I suppose you can arrange transportation for me to Srinigar V."

"I can't even afford to go to Nagóndicon," Flaswell said. "I will inform Roebuck-Ward of their error. They will undoubtedly arrange transportation for you, when they send me my Frontier Model Bride."

Sheila shrugged her shoulders. "Travel broadens one," she said.

Flaswell nodded. He was thinking hard. This girl had, it was obvious, no pioneering qualities. But she was amazingly pretty. He saw no reason why her stay shouldn't be a pleasant one for both.

"Under the circumstances," Flaswell said, with an ingratiating smile, "we might as well be friends."

"Under what circumstances?"

"We are the only two Human People on the planet." Flaswell rested a hand lightly on her shoulder. "Let's have a drink. Tell me all about yourself. Do you—"

At that moment, he heard a loud sound behind. He turned and saw a small, squat robot climbing from a compartment in the packing case.

"What do you want?" Flaswell demanded.

"I," said the robot, "am a Marrying Robot, empowered by the government to provide legal marriages in space. I am further directed by the Roebuck-Ward Company to act as guardian, duenna and protector for the young lady in my charge, until such time as my primary function, to perform a ceremony of marriage, has been accomplished."

"Uppity damned robot," Flaswell grumbled.

"What did you expect?" Sheila asked. "A quick-frozen Human preacher?"

"Of course not. But a robot duenna—"

"The very best kind," she assured him. "You'd be surprised at how some men act when they get a few light-years from Earth."

"I would?" Flaswell said disconsolately.

"So I'm told," Sheila replied, demurely looking away from him. "And after all, the promised bride of the Pasha of Srae should have a guardian of some sort."

"Dearly beloved," the robot intoned, "we are here gathered to join—"

"Not now," Sheila said loftily. "Not this one."

"I'll have the robots fix a room for you," Flaswell growled, and walked away, mumbling to himself about Human Man's Burden.

He radioed Roebuck-Ward and was told that the proper

model Bride would be sent at once and the interloper shipped
elsewhere. Then he returned to his farming and mining, determined to ignore the presence of Sheila and her duenna.

Work continued on Chance. There was thorium to be
mined out of the soil and new wells to dig. Harvest time was
soon at hand, and the robots toiled for long hours in the green-
blossomed fields, and lubricating oil glistened on their honest
metal faces, and the air was fragrant with the perfume of the
dir flowers.

Sheila made her presence felt with subtle yet surprising
force. Soon there were plastic lampshades over the naked cold-
light bulbs and drapes over the stark windows and scatter rugs
on the floors. And there were many other changes around the
house that Flaswell felt rather than saw.

His diet underwent a change, too. The robot chef's memory
tape had worn thin in many spots, so all the poor mechanical
could remember how to make was beef Stroganoff, cucumber
salad, rice pudding and cocoa. Flaswell had, with considerable
stoicism, been eating these dishes ever since he came to
Chance, varying them occasionally with shipwreck rations.

Then Sheila took the robot chef in hand. Patiently she
impressed upon his memory tape the receipts for beef stew,
pot roast, tossed green salad, apple pie, and many others. The
eating situation upon Chance began to improve markedly.

But when Sheila put up smis jelly in vacuum jars, Flaswell
began to have doubts.

Here, after all, was a remarkably practical young lady, in
spite of her expensive appearance. She could do all the things
a Frontier Wife could do. And she had other attributes. What
did he need a regular Roebuck-Ward Frontier Model for?

After mulling this for a while, Flaswell said to his foreman,
"Gunga-Sam, I am confused."

"Ah?" said the foreman, his metal face impassive.

"I guess I need a little of that robot intuition. She's doing
very well, isn't she, Gunga-Sam?"

"The Human Woman is taking her proper share of Human
Person's Burden."

"She sure is. But can it last? She's doing as much as any
Frontier Model Wife could do, isn't she? Cooking, can-
ning—"

"The workers love her," Gunga-Sam said with simple
dignity. "You did not know, sir, but when that rust epidemic
broke out last week, she toiled night and day, bringing relief
and comforting the frightened younger robots."

"She did all that?" Flaswell gasped, shaken. "But a girl of her background, a luxury model—"

"It does not matter. She is a Human Person and she has the strength and nobility to take on Human Person's Burden."

"Do you know," Flaswell said slowly, "this has convinced me. I really believe she is fit to stay here. It's not her fault she isn't a Frontier Model. That's a matter of screening and conditioning, and you can't change that. I'm going to tell her she can stay. And then I'll cancel the other Roebuck order."

A strange expression glowed in the foreman's eyes, an expression almost of amusement. He bowed low and said, "It shall be as the master wishes."

Flaswell hurried out to find Sheila.

She was in the sick bay, which had been constructed out of an old toolshed. With the aid of a robot mechanic, she was caring for the dents and dislocations that are the peculiar lot of metal-skinned beings.

"Sheila," Flaswell said, "I want to speak to you."

"Sure," she answered absently, "as soon as I tighten this bolt."

She locked the bolt cleverly into place, and tapped the robot with her wrench.

"There, Pedro," she said, "try that leg now."

The robot stood up gingerly, put weight on the leg, found that it held. He capered comically around the Human Woman, saying, "You sure fixed it, Boss Lady. Gracias, ma'am."

And he danced out into the sunshine.

Flaswell and Sheila watched him go, smiling at his antics. "They're just like children," Flaswell said.

"One can't help but love them," Sheila responded. "They're so happy, so carefree—"

"But they haven't got souls," Flaswell reminded her.

"No," she agreed somberly. "They haven't. What did you wish to see me about?"

"I wanted to tell you—" Flaswell looked around. The sick bay was an antiseptic place, filled with wrenches, screwdrivers, hacksaws, ballpeen hammers and other medical equipment. It was hardly the atmosphere for the sort of announcement he was about to make.

"Come with me," he said.

They walked out of the hospital and through the blossoming green fields, to the foot of Flaswell's spectacular mountains. There, shadowed by craggy cliffs, was a still, dark pool of water overhung with giant trees, which Flaswell had force-grown. Here they paused.

"I wanted to say this," Flaswell said. "You have surprised me completely, Sheila. I expected you would be a parasite, a purposeless person. Your background, your breeding, your appearance all pointed in this direction. But I was wrong. You have risen to the challenge of a Frontier environment, have conquered it triumphantly, and have won the hearts of everybody."

"Everybody?" Sheila asked very softly.

"I believe I can speak for every robot on the planetoid. They idolize you. I think you belong here, Sheila."

The girl was silent for a long while, and the wind murmured through the boughs of the giant force-grown trees, and ruffled the black surface of the lake.

Finally she said, "Do you think I belong here?"

Flaswell felt engulfed by her exquisite perfection, lost in the topaz depths of her eyes. His breath came fast, he touched her hand, her fingers clung.

"Sheila. . . ."

"Yes, Edward. . . ."

"Dearly beloved," a strident metallic voice barked, "we are here gathered—"

"Not now, you fool!" Sheila cried.

The Marrying Robot came forward and said sulkily, "Much as I hate to interfere in the affairs of Human People, my taped coefficients are such that I must. To my way of thinking, physical contact is meaningless. I have, by way of experiment, clashed limbs with a seamstress robot. All I got for my troubles was a dent. Once I thought I experienced something, an electric something that shot through me giddily and made me think of slowly shifting geometric forms. But upon examination, I discovered the insulation had parted from a conductor center. Therefore, the emotion was invalid."

"Uppity damned robot," Flaswell growled.

"Excuse my presumption. I was merely trying to explain that I personally find my instructions unintelligible—that is, to prevent any and all physical contact until a ceremony of marriage has been performed. But there it is; those are my orders. Can't I get it over with now?'

"No!" said Sheila.

The robot shrugged his shoulders fatalistically and slid into the underbrush.

"Can't stand a robot who doesn't know his place," said Flaswell. "But it's all right."

"What?"

"Yes," Flaswell said, with an air of conviction. "You are as good as any Frontier Model Wife and far prettier. Sheila, will you marry me?"

The robot, who had been thrashing around in the underbrush, now slid eagerly toward them.

"No," said Sheila.

"No?" Flaswell repeated uncomprehendingly.

"You heard me. No! Absolutely no!"

"But why? You fit so well here, Sheila. The robots adore you. I've never seen them work so well—"

"I'm not interested in your robots," she said, standing very straight, her hair disheveled, her eyes blazing. "And I am not interested in your planetoid. And I am most emphatically not interested in you. I am going to Srinigar V, where I will be the pampered bride of the Pasha of Srae!"

They stared at each other, Sheila white-faced with anger, Flaswell red with confusion.

The Marrying Robot said, "Now should I start the ceremony? Dearly beloved. . . ."

Sheila whirled and ran toward the house.

"I don't understand," the Marrying Robot said plaintively. "It's all very bewildering. When does the ceremony take place?"

"It doesn't," Flaswell said, and stalked toward the house, his brows beetling with rage.

The robot hesitated, sighed metallically and hurried after the Ultra Deluxe Luxury Model Bride.

All that night, Flaswell sat in his room, drank deeply and mumbled to himself. Shortly after dawn, the loyal Gunga-Sam knocked and slipped into the room.

"Women!" Flaswell snarled to his servitor.

"Ah?" said Gunga-Sam.

"I'll never understand them," Flaswell said. "She led me on. I thought she wanted to stay here. I thought. . . ."

"The mind of Human Man is murky and dark," said Gunga-Sam, "but it is as crystal compared to the mind of Human Woman."

"Where did you get that?" Flaswell asked.

"It is an ancient robot proverb."

"You robots. Sometimes I wonder if you *don't* have souls."

"Oh, no, Mr. Flaswell, Boss. It is expressly written in our Construction Specifications that robots are to be built with no souls, to spare them anguish."

"A very wise provision," Flaswell said, "and something they might consider with Human People, too. Well, to hell with her. What do you want?"

"I came to tell you, sir, that the drone freighter is landing."

Flaswell turned pale. "So soon? Then it's bringing my new bride!"

"Undoubtedly."

"And it will take Sheila away to Srinigar V."

"Assuredly, sir."

Flaswell groaned and clutched his head. Then he straightened and said, "All right, all right. I'll see if she's ready."

He found Sheila in the living room, watching the drone freighter spiral in. She said, "The very best of luck, Edward. I hope your new bride fulfills all your expectations."

The drone freighter landed and the robots began removing a large packing case.

"I had better go," Sheila said. "They won't wait long." She held out her hand.

Flaswell took it.

He held her hand for a moment, then found he was holding her arm. She did not resist, nor did the Marrying Robot break into the room. Flaswell suddenly found that Sheila was in his arms. He kissed her and felt exactly like a small sun going nova.

Finally she said, "Wow," huskily, in a not quite believing voice.

Flaswell cleared his throat twice. "Sheila, I love you. I can't offer you much luxury here, but if you'd stay—"

"It's about time you found out you loved me, you dope!" she said. "Of course I'm staying!"

The next few minutes were ecstatic and decidedly vertiginous. They were interrupted at last by the sound of loud robot voices outside. The door burst open and the Marrying Robot stamped in, followed by Gunga-Sam and two farm mechanicals.

"Really!" the Marrying Robot said. "It is unbelievable! To think I'd see the day when robot pitted himself against robot!"

"What happened?" Flaswell asked.

"This foreman of yours *sat* on me," the Marrying Robot said indignantly, "while his cronies held my limbs. I was merely trying to enter this room and perform my duty as set forth by the government and the Roebuck-Ward Company."

"Why, Gunga-Sam!" Flaswell said, grinning.

The Marrying Robot hurried up to Sheila. "Are you damaged? Any dents? Any short-circuits?"

"I don't think so," said Sheila breathlessly.

Gunga-Sam said to Flaswell, 'The fault is all mine, Boss, sir. But everyone knows that Human Man and Human Woman need solitude during the courtship period. I merely performed what I considered my duty to the Human Race in this respect, Mr. Flaswell, Boss, sahib."

"You did well, Gunga-Sam," Flaswell said. "I'm deeply grateful and—oh, Lord!"

"What is it?" Sheila asked apprehensively.

Flaswell was staring out the window. The farm robots were carrying the large packing case toward the house."

"The Frontier Model Bride!" said Flaswell. "What'll we do, darling? I canceled you and legally contracted for the other one. Do you think we can break the contract?"

Sheila laughed. "Don't worry. There's no Frontier Model Bride in that box. Your order was canceled as soon as it was received."

"It was?"

"Certainly." She looked down, ashamed. "You'll hate me for this—"

"I won't," he promised. "What is it?"

"Well, Frontiersmen's pictures are on file at the Company, you know, so Brides can see what they're getting. There is a choice—for the girls, I mean—and I'd been hanging around the place so long, unable to get unclassified as an Ultra Deluxe, that I—I made friends with the head of the order department. And," she said all in a rush, "I got myself sent here."

"But the Pasha of Srae—"

"I made him up."

"But why?" Flaswell asked puzzledly. "You're so pretty—"

"That everybody expects me to be a toy for some spoiled, pudgy idiot," she finished with a good deal of heat. "I don't want to be! I want to be a wife! And I'm just as good as any chunky, homely female!"

"Better," he said.

"I can cook and doctor robots and be practical, can't I? Haven't I proved it?"

"Of course, dear."

She began to cry. "But nobody would believe it, so I had to trick you into letting me stay long enough to—to fall in love with me."

"Which I did," he said, drying her eyes for her. "It's all worked out fine. The whole thing was a lucky accident."

What looked like a blush appeared on Gunga-Sam's metallic face.

"You mean it wasn't an accident?" Flaswell exclaimed.

"Well, sir, Mr. Flaswell, effendi, it is well known that Human Man needs attractive Human Woman. The Frontier Model sounded a little severe and Memsahib Sheila is a daughter of a friend of my former master. So I took the liberty of sending the order directly to her. She got her friend in the order department to show her your picture and ship her here. I hope you are not displeased with your humble servant for disobeying."

"Well, I'll be damned," Flaswell finally got out. "It's like I always said—you robots understand Human People better than anyone." He turned to Sheila. "But what *is* in that packing case?"

"My dresses and my jewelry, my shoes, my cosmetics, my hair styler, my—"

"But—"

"You want me to look nice when we go visiting, dear," Sheila said. "After all, Cythera III is only fifteen days away. I looked it up before I came."

Flaswell nodded resignedly. You had to expect something like this from an Ultra Deluxe Luxury Model Bride.

"Now!" Sheila said, turning to the Marrying Robot.

The robot didn't answer.

"Now!" Flaswell shouted.

"You're quite sure?" the robot queried sulkily.

"Yes! Get started!"

"I just don't understand," the Marrying Robot said. "Why now? Why not last week? Am I the only sane one here? Oh, well. Dearly beloved. . . ."

And the ceremony was held at last. Flaswell proclaimed a three day holiday and the robots sang and danced and celebrated in their carefree robot fashion.

Thereafter, life was never the same on Chance. The Flaswells began to have a modest social life, to visit and be visited by couples fifteen and twenty days out, on Cythera III, Tham and Randico I. But the rest of the time, Sheila was an irreproachable Frontier Wife, loved by the robots and idolized by her husband. The Marrying Robot, following his instruction manual, retrained himself as an accountant and bookkeeper, skills for which his mentality was peculiarly well suited. He often said the whole place would go to pieces if it weren't for him.

And the robots continued to dig thorium from the soil, and the dir, olge and smis blossoned, and Flaswell and Sheila shared together the responsibility of Human People's Burden.

Flaswell was aways quite vocal on the advantages of shopping at Roebuck-Ward. But Sheila knew that the real advantage was in having a foreman like the loyal, soulless Gunga-Sam.

FEAR IN THE
NIGHT

She heard herself screaming as she woke up and knew she must have been screaming for long seconds. It was cold in the room but she was covered with perspiration; it rolled down her face and shoulders, down the front of her nightgown. Her back was damp with sweat and the sheet beneath her was damp.

Immediately she began to shiver.

"Are you all right?" her husband asked.

For a few moments she couldn't answer. Her knees were drawn up and she coiled her arms tightly around them, trying to stop shuddering. Her husband was a dark mass beside her, a long dark cylinder against the faintly glimmering sheet. Looking at him, she began trembling again.

"Will it help if I snap on the light?" he asked.

"No!" she said sharply. "Don't move—please!"

And then there was only the steady ticking of the clock, but somehow that was filled with menace also.

"Did it happen again?"

"Yes," she said. "Just the same. For Lord's sake, don't touch me!" He had started to move toward her, dark and sinuous against the sheet, and she was trembling, violently again.

"The dream," he began cautiously, "was it . . . was I . . . ?" Delicately, he left it unvoiced, shifting his position on the bed slightly, carefully so she wouldn't be frightened.

But she was getting a grip on herself again. She unclenched her hands, putting the palms hard and flat against the bed.

"Yes," she said. "The snakes again. They were crawling all over me. Big ones and little ones, hundreds of them. The room was filled with them and more were coming in the door, through the windows. The closet was filled with snakes, so full they were coming under the door onto the floor—"

"Easy," he said. "Sure you want to talk about it?"

She didn't answer.

"Want the light on yet?" he asked her gently.

She hesitated, then said, "Not yet. I don't dare just yet."

"Oh," he said in a tone of complete understanding. "Then the other part of the dream—"

"Yes."

"Look, perhaps you shouldn't talk about it."

"Let's talk about it." She tried to laugh but it came out a cough. "You'd think I'd be getting used to it. For how many nights now?"

The dream always began with the little snake, slowly crawling across her arm, watching her with evil red eyes. She flung it from her, sitting up in bed. Then another slithered across the covers, fatter, faster. She flung that one away too, getting quickly out of bed and standing on the floor. Then there was one under her foot and then one was coiled in her hair, over her eyes, and through the now-opened door came still more, forcing her back on the bed, screaming, reaching for her husband.

But in the dream her husband wasn't there. In the bed beside her, a long dark cylinder against the faintly glimmering sheets, was a tremendous snake. She didn't realize it until her arms were around it.

"Turn on the light now," she commanded. Her muscles contracted, straining against each other as light flooded the room. Her thighs tensed, ready to hurl her out of bed if . . .

But it was her husband after all.

"Dear Lord," she breathed and relaxed completely, sagging against the mattress.

"Surprised?" he asked her, grinning wryly.

"Each time," she told him, "each time I'm sure you won't be there. I'm sure there'll be a snake there." She touched his arm just to make sure.

"You see how foolish it all is?" he said softly, soothingly.

"If you would only forget. If you would only have confidence in me these nightmares would pass."

"I know," she said, drinking in the details of the room. The little telephone table was immensely reassuring with its litter of scribbled lists and messages. The scarred mahogany bureau was an old friend, as was the little radio and the newspaper on the floor. And how sane her emerald-green dress was, thrown carelessly across the slipper chair!

"The doctor told you the same thing," he said. "When we were having our trouble you associated me with everything that went wrong, everything that hurt you. And now that our troubles are over, you still do."

"Not consciously," she said, "I swear, not consciously."

"But you do all the same," he insisted. "Remember when I wanted the divorce? When I told you I'd never loved you? Remember how you hated me then, even though you wouldn't let me go?" He paused for breath. "You hated Helen and me. That has taken its toll. The hate has remained under our reconciliation."

"I don't believe I ever hated you," she said. "Only Helen —that skinny little monkey!"

"Mustn't speak ill of those departed from trouble," he murmured.

"Yes," she said thoughtfully. "I suppose I drove her to that breakdown. I can't say I'm sorry. Do you think she's haunting me?"

"You mustn't blame yourself," he said. "She was high-strung, nervous, artistic. A neurotic type."

"I'll get over all this now that Helen's gone." She smiled at him and the lines of worry on her forehead vanished. "I'm so crazy about you," she murmured, running her fingers through his light-brown hair. "I'd never let you go."

"You'd better not." He smiled back at her. "I don't want to go."

"Just help me."

"With all I've got." He bent forward and kissed her lightly on the cheek. "But, darling, unless you get over these nightmares—featuring me as the principal villain—I'll have to—"

"Don't say it," she murmured quickly. "I can't bear the thought. And we are past the bad time."

He nodded.

"You're right, though," she said, "I think I'll try a different psychiatrist. I can't stand much more of this. These dreams, night after night."

"And they're getting worse," he reminded her, frowning. "At first it was only once in a while but now it's every night. Soon, if you don't do something, it'll be—"

"All right," she said. "Don't talk about it."

"I have to. I'm getting worried. If this snake fixation keeps up, you'll be taking a knife to me while I'm asleep one of these nights."

"Never," she told him. "But don't talk about it. I want to forget it. I don't think it'll happen again. Do you?"

"I hope not," he said.

She reached across him and turned off the light, kissed him and closed her eyes.

After a few minutes she turned over on her side. In half

an hour she rolled over again, said something incoherent and was quiet. After twenty minutes more she had shrugged one shoulder but, other than that, made no motion.

Her husband was a dark mass beside her, propped up on one elbow. He lay in the darkness, thinking, listening to her breathe, hearing the tick of the clock. Then he stretched out at full length.

Slowly he untied the cord of his pajamas and pulled until he had a foot of it free. Then he drew back the covers. Very gently he rolled toward her with the cord in his hand, listening to her breathing. He placed the cord against her arm. Slowly, allowing himself seconds to an inch, he pulled the cord along her arm.

Presently she moaned.

BAD
MEDICINE

On May 2, 2103, Elwood Caswell walked rapidly down Broadway with a loaded revolver hidden in his coat pocket. He didn't want to use the weapon, but feared he might anyhow. This was a justifiable assumption, for Caswell was a homicidal maniac.

It was a gentle, misty spring day and the air held the smell of rain and blossoming dogwood. Caswell gripped the revolver in his sweaty right hand and tried to think of a single valid reason why he should not kill a man named Magnessen, who, the other day, had commented on how well Caswell looked.

What business was it of Magnessen's how he looked? Damned busybodies, always spoiling things for everybody. . .

Caswell was a choleric little man with fierce red eyes, bulldog jowls and ginger-red hair. He was the sort you would expect to find perched on a detergent box, orating to a crowd of lunching businessmen and amused students, shouting, "Mars for the Martians, Venus for the Venusians!"

But in truth, Caswell was uninterested in the deplorable social conditions of extraterrestrials. He was a jetbus conductor for the New York Rapid Transit Corporation. He minded his own business. And he was quite mad.

Fortunately, he knew this at least part of the time, with at least half of his mind.

Perspiring freely, Caswell continued down Broadway toward the 43rd Street branch of Home Therapy Appliances, Inc. His friend Magnessen would be finishing work soon, returning to his little apartment less than a block from Caswell's. How easy it would be, how pleasant, to saunter in, exchange a few words and . . .

No! Caswell took a deep gulp of air and reminded himself that he didn't *really* want to kill anyone. It was not right to kill people. The authorities would lock him up, his friends wouldn't understand, his mother would never have approved.

But these arguments seemed pallid, over-intellectual and

entirely without force. The simple fact remained—he wanted to kill Magnessen.

Could so strong a desire be wrong? Or even unhealthy?

Yes, it could! With an agonized groan, Caswell sprinted the last few steps into the Home Therapy Appliances Store.

Just being within such a place gave him an immediate sense of relief. The lighting was discreet, the draperies were neutral, the displays of glittering therapy machines were neither too bland nor obstreperous. It was the kind of place where a man could happily lie down on the carpet in the shadow of the therapy machines, secure in the knowledge that help for any sort of trouble was at hand.

A clerk with fair hair and a long, supercilious nose glided up softly, but not too softly, and murmured, "May one help?"

"Therapy!" said Caswell.

"Of course, sir," the clerk answered, smoothing his lapels and smiling winningly. "That is what we are here for." He gave Caswell a searching look, performed an instant mental diagnosis, and tapped a gleaming white-and-copper machine.

"Now this," the clerk said, "is the new Alcoholic Reliever, built by IBM and advertised in the leading magazines. A handsome piece of furniture, I think you will agree, and not out of place in any home. It opens into a television set."

With a flick of his narrow wrist, the clerk opened the Alcoholic Reliever, revealing a 52-inch screen.

"I need—" Caswell began.

"Therapy," the clerk finished for him. "Of course. I just wanted to point out that this model need never cause embarrassment for yourself, your friends or loved ones. Notice, if you will, the recessed dial which controls the desired degree of drinking. See? If you do not wish total abstinence, you can set it to heavy, moderate, social or light. That is a new feature, unique in mechanotherapy."

"I am not an alcoholic," Caswell said, with considerable dignity. "The New York Rapid Transit Corporation does not hire alcoholics."

"Oh," said the clerk, glancing distrustfully at Caswell's bloodshot eyes. "You seem a little nervous. Perhaps the portable Bendix Anxiety Reducer—"

"Anxiety's not my ticket, either. What have you got for homicidal mania?"

The clerk pursed his lips. "Schizophrenic or manic-depressive origins?"

"I don't know," Caswell admitted, somewhat taken aback.

"It really doesn't matter," the clerk told him. "Just a private theory of my own. From my experience in the store, redheads and blonds are prone to schizophrenia, while brunettes incline toward the manic-depressive."

"That's interesting. Have you worked here long?"

"A week. Now then, here is just what you need, sir." He put his hand affectionately on a squat black machine with chrome trim.

"What's that?"

"That, sir, is the Rex Regenerator, built by General Motors. Isn't it handsome? It can go with any decor and opens up into a well-stocked bar. Your friends, family, loved ones need never know—"

"Will it cure a homicidal urge?" Caswell asked. "A *strong* one?"

"Absolutely. Don't confuse this with the little ten amp neurosis models. This is a hefty, heavy-duty, twenty-five amp machine for a really deep-rooted major condition."

"That's what I've got," said Caswell, with pardonable pride.

"This baby'll jolt it out of you. Big, heavy-duty thrust bearings! Oversize heat absorbers! Completely insulated! Sensitivity range of over—"

"I'll take it," Caswell said. "Right now. I'll pay cash."

"Fine! I'll just telephone Storage and—"

"This one'll do," Caswell said, pulling out his billfold. "I'm in a hurry to use it. I want to kill my friend Magnessen, you know."

The clerk clucked sympathetically. "You wouldn't want to do that. . . . Plus five per cent sales tax. Thank you, sir. Full instructions are inside."

Caswell thanked him, lifted the Regenerator in both arms and hurried out.

After figuring his commission, the clerk smiled to himself and lighted a cigarette. His enjoyment was spoiled when the manager, a large man impressively equipped with pince-nez, marched out of his office.

"Haskins," the manager said, "I thought I asked you to rid yourself of that filthy habit."

"Yes, Mr. Follansby, sorry, sir," Haskins apologized, snubbing out the cigarette. "I'll use the display Denicotinizer at once. Made rather a good sale, Mr. Follansby. One of the big Rex Regenerators."

"Really?" said the manager, impressed. "It isn't often we— wait a minute! You didn't sell the *floor model*, did you?"

"Why—why, I'm afraid I did, Mr. Follansby. The customer was in such a terrible hurry. Was there any reason—"

Mr. Follansby gripped his promiinent white forehead in both hands, as though he wished to rip it off. "Haskins, I told you. I must have told you! That display Regenerator was a Martian model. For giving mechanotherapy to Martians."

"Oh," Haskins said. He thought for a moment. "Oh."

Mr. Follansby stared at his clerk in grim silence.

"But does it really matter?" Haskins asked quickly. "Surely the machine won't discriminate. I should think it would treat a homicidal tendency even if the patient were not a Martian."

"The Martian race has never had the slightest tendency toward homicide. A Martian Regenerator doesn't even possess the concept. Of course the Regenerator will treat him. It has to. But *what will it treat?*"

"Oh," said Haskins.

"That poor devil must be stopped before—you say he was homicidal? I don't know what will happen! Quick, what is his address?"

"Well, Mr. Follansby, he was in such a terrible hurry—"

The manager gave him a long, unbelieving look. "Get the police! Call the General Motors Security Division! Find him!"

Haskins raced for the door.

"Wait!" yelled the manager, struggling into a raincoat. "I'm coming, too!"

Elwood Caswell returned to his apartment by taxicopter. He lugged the Regenerator into his living room, put it down near the couch and studied it thoughtfully.

"That clerk was right," he said after a while. "It *does* go with the room."

Esthetically, the Regenerator was a success.

Caswell admired it for a few more moments, then went into the kitchen and fixed himself a chicken sandwich. He ate slowly, staring fixedly at a point just above and to the left of his kitchen clock.

Damn you, Magnessen! Dirty no-good lying shifty-eyed enemy of all that's decent and clean in the world. . .

Taking the revolver from his pocket, he laid it on the table. With a stiffened forefinger, he poked it into different positions.

It was time to begin therapy.

Except that. . .

Caswell realized worriedly that he didn't want to lose the desire to kill Magnessen. What would become of him if he lost that urge? His life would lose all purpose, all coherence, all flavor and zest. It would be quite dull, really.

Moreover, he had a great and genuine grievance against Magnessen, one he didn't like to think about.

Irene!

His poor sister, debauched by the subtle and insidious Magnessen, ruined by him and cast aside. What better reason could a man have to take his revolver and . . .

Caswell finally remembered that he did not have a sister.

Now was really the time to begin therapy.

He went into the living room and found the operating instructions tucked into a ventilation louver of the machine. He opened them and read:

To Operate All Rex Model Regenerators:

1. Place the Regenerator near a comfortable couch. (A comfortable couch can be purchased as an additional accessory from any General Motors dealer.)

2. Plug in the machine.

3. Affix the adjustable contact-band to the forehead.

And that's all! Your Regenerator will do the rest! There will be no language bar or dialect problem, since the Regenerator communicates by Direct Sense Contact (Patent Pending). All you must do is cooperate.

Try not to feel any embarrassment or shame. Everyone has problems and many are worse than yours! Your Regenerator has no interest in your morals or ethical standards, so don't feel it is 'judging' you. It desires only to aid you in becoming well and happy.

As soon as it has collected and processed enough data, your Regenerator will begin treatment. You make the sessions as short or as long as you like. You are the boss! And of course you can end a session at any time.

That's all there is to it! Simple, isn't it? Now plug in your General Motors Regenerator and GET SANE!

"Nothing hard about that," Cassidy said to himself. He pushed the Regenerator closer to the couch and plugged it in. He lifted the headband, started to slip it on, stopped.

"I feel so silly!" he giggled.

Abruptly he closed his mouth and stared pugnaciously at the black-and-chrome machine.

"So you think you can make me sane, huh?"

The Regenerator didn't answer.

"Oh, well, go ahead and try." He slipped the headband over his forehead, crossed his arms on his chest and leaned back.

Nothing happened. Caswell settled himself more comfortably on the couch. He scratched his shoulder and put the headband at a more comfortable angle. Still nothing. His thoughts began to wander.

Magnessen! You noisy, overbearing oaf, you disgusting—

"Good afternoon," a voice murmured in his head. "I am your mechanotherapist."

Caswell twitched guiltily. "Hello. I was just—you know, just sort of—"

"Of course," the machine said soothingly. "Don't we all? I am now scanning the material in your preconscious with the intent of synthesis, diagnosis, prognosis and treatment. I find . . ."

"Yes?"

"Just one moment." The Regenerator was silent for several minutes. Then, hesitantly, it said, "This is beyond doubt a most unusual case."

"Really?" Cassidy asked, pleased.

"Yes. The coefficients seem—I'm not sure. . ." The machine's robotic voice grew feeble. The pilot light began to flicker and fade.

"Hey, what's the matter?"

"Confusion," said the machine. "Of course," it went on in a stronger voice, "the unusual nature of the symptoms need not prove entirely baffling to a competent therapeutic machine. A symptom, no matter how bizarre, is no more than a signpost, an indication of inner difficulty. And *all* symptoms can be related to the broad mainstream of proven theory. Since the theory is effective, the symptoms must relate. We will proceed on that assumption."

"Are you sure you know what you're doing?" asked Caswell, feeling light-headed.

The machine snapped back, its pilot light blazing, "Mechanotherapy today is an exact science and admits no significant errors. We will proceed with a word-association test."

"Fire away," said Caswell.

"House?"

"Home."

"Dog?"

"Cat."

"Fleefl?"

Caswell hesitated, trying to figure out the word. It sounded vaguely Martian, but it might be Venusian or even—

"Fleefl?" the Regenerator repeated.

"Marfoosh," Caswell replied, making up the word on the spur of the moment.

"Loud?"

"Sweet."

"Green?"

"Mother."

"Thanagoyes?"

"Patamathonga."

"Arrides?"

"Nexothesmodrastica."

"Chtheesnohelgnopteces?"

"Rigamaroo latasentricpropatria!" Caswell shot back. It was a collection of sounds he was particularly proud of. The average man would not have been able to pronounce them.

"Hmm," said the Regenerator. "The pattern fits. It always does."

"What pattern?"

"You have," the machine informed him, "a classic case of feem desire, complicated by strong dwarkish intentions."

"I do? I thought I was homicidal."

"That term has no referent," the machine said severely. "Therefore I must reject it as nonsense syllabification. Now consider these points: The feem desire is perfectly normal. Never forget that. But it is usually replaced at an early age by the hovendish revulsion. Individuals lacking in this basic environmental response—"

"I'm not absolutely sure I know what you're talking about," Caswell confessed.

"Please, sir! We must establish one thing at once. You are the patient. I am the mechanotherapist. You have brought your troubles to me for treatment. But you cannot expect help unless you cooperate."

"All right," Caswell said. "I'll try."

Up to now, he had been bathed in a warm glow of superiority. Everything the machine said had seemed mildly humorous. As a matter of fact, he had felt capable of pointing out a few things wrong with the mechanotherapist.

Now that sense of well-being evaporated, as it always did, and Caswell was alone, terribly alone and lost, a creature of his compulsions, in search of a little peace and contentment. He would undergo anything to find them. Sternly he reminded himself that he had no right to comment on the mechanotherapist. These machines knew what they were doing and had been doing it for a long time. He would cooperate, no matter how outlandish the treatment seemed from his layman's viewpoint.

But it was obvious, Caswell thought, settling himself grimly on the couch, that mechanotherapy was going to be far more difficult than he had imagined.

The search for the missing customer had been brief and useless. He was nowhere to be found on the teeming New York streets and no one could remember seeing a red-haired, red-eyed little man lugging a black therapeutic machine.

It was all too common a sight.

In answer to an urgent telephone call, the police came immediately, four of them, led by a harassed young lieutenant of detectives named Smith.

Smith just had time to ask, "Say, why don't you people put tags on things?" when there was an interruption.

A man pushed his way past the policeman at the door. He was tall and gnarled and ugly, and his eyes were deep-set and bleakly blue. His clothes, unpressed and uncaring, hung on him like corrugated iron.

"What do you want?" Lieutenant Smith asked.

The ugly man flipped back his lapel, showing a small silver badge beneath. "I'm John Rath," General Motors Security Division."

"Oh. . . Sorry, sir," Lieutenant Smith said, saluting. "I didn't think you people would move in so fast."

Rath made a noncommittal noise. "Have you checked for prints, Lieutenant? The customer might have touched some other therapy machine."

"I'll get right on it, sir," Smith said. It wasn't often that one of the operatives from GM, GE or IBM came down to take a personal hand. If a local cop showed he was really clicking, there just might be the possibility of an Industrial Transfer. . .

Rath turned to Follansby and Haskins, and transfixed them with a gaze as piercing and as impersonal as a radar beam. "Let's have the full story," he said, taking a notebook and pencil from a shapeless pocket.

He listened to the tale in ominous silence. Finally he closed his notebook, thrust it back into his pocket and said, "The therapeutic machines are a sacred trust. To give a customer the wrong machine is a betrayal of that trust, a violation of the Public Interest, and a defamation of the Company's good reputation."

The manager nodded in agreement, glaring at his unhappy clerk.

"A Martian model," Rath continued, "should never have been on the floor in the first place."

"I can explain that," Follansby said hastily. "We needed a demonstrator model and I wrote to the Company, telling them—"

"This might," Rath broke in inexorably, "be considered a case of gross criminal negligence."

Both the manager and the clerk exchanged horrified looks. They were thinking of the General Motors Reformatory outside of Detroit, where Company offenders passed their days in sullen silence, monotonously drawing micro-circuits for pocket television sets.

"However, that is out of my jurisdiction," Rath said. He turned his baleful gaze full upon Haskins. "You are certain that the customer never mentioned his name?"

"No, sir. I mean yes, I'm sure," Haskins replied rattledly.

"Did he mention any names at all?"

Haskins plunged his face into his hands. He looked up and said eagerly, "Yes! He wanted to kill someone! A friend of his!"

"Who?" Rath asked, with terrible patience.

"The friend's name was—let me think—Magneton! That was it! Magneton! Or was it Morrison? Oh, dear . . ."

Mr. Rath's iron face registered a rather corrugated disgust. People were useless as witnesses. Worse than useless, since they were frequently misleading. For reliability, give him a robot every time.

"Didn't he mention *anything* significant?"

"Let me *think!*" Haskins said, his face twisting into a fit of concentration.

Rath waited.

Mr. Follansby cleared his throat. "I was just thinking, Mr. Rath. About that Martian machine. It won't treat a Terran homicidal case as homicidal, will it?"

"Of course not. Homicide is unknown on Mars."

"Yes. But what will it do? Might it not reject the entire case as unsuitable? Then the customer would merely return the Regenerator with a complaint and we would—"

Mr. Rath shook his head. "The Rex Regenerator must treat if it finds evidence of psychosis. By Martian standards, the customer is a very sick man, a psychotic—*no matter what is wrong with him.*"

Follansby removed his pince-nez and polished them rapidly. "What will the machine do, then?"

"It will treat him for the Martian illness most analogous to his case. Feem desire, I should imagine, with various complications. As for what will happen once treatment begins, I don't know. I doubt whether anyone knows, since it has never happened before. Offhand, I would say there are two major alternatives: The patient may reject the therapy out of hand, in which case he is left with his homicidal mania unabated. Or he may accept the Martian therapy and reach a cure."

Mr. Follansby's face brightened. "Ah! A cure is possible!"

"You don't understand," Rath said. "He may effect a cure—*of his non-existent Martian psychosis.* But to cure something that is not there is, in effect, to erect a gratuitous delusional system. You might say that the machine would work in reverse, producing psychosis instead of removing it."

Mr. Follansby groaned and leaned against a Bell Psychosomatica.

"The result," Rath summed up, "would be to convince the customer that he was a Martian. A sane Martian, naturally."

Haskins suddenly shouted, "I remember! I remember now! He said he worked for the New York Rapid Transit Corporation! I remember distinctly!"

"That's a break," Rath said, reaching for the telephone.

Haskins wiped his perspiring face in relief. "And I just remembered something else that should make it easier still."

"What?"

"The customer said he had been an alcoholic at one time. I'm sure of it, because he was interested at first in the IBM Alcoholic Reliever, until I talked him out of it. He had red hair, you know, and I've had a theory for some time about red-headedness and alcoholism. It seems—"

"Excellent," Rath said. "Alcoholism will be on his records. It narrows the search considerably."

As he dialed the NYRT Corporation, the expression on his craglike face was almost pleasant.

It was good, for a change, to find that a human *could* retain some significant facts.

"But surely you remember your goricae?" the Regenerator was saying.

"No," Caswell answered wearily.

"Tell me, then, about your juvenile experiences with the thorastrian fleep."

"Never had any."

"Hmm. Blockage," muttered the machine. "Resentment. Repression. Are you sure you don't remember your goricae and what it meant to you? The experience is universal."

"Not for me," Caswell said, swallowing a yawn.

He had been undergoing mechanotherapy for close to four hours and it struck him as futile. For a while, he had talked voluntarily about his childhood, his mother and father, his older brother. But the Regenerator had asked him to put aside those fantasies. The patient's relationships to an imaginary parent or sibling, it explained, were unworkable and of minor importance psychologically. The important thing was the patient's feelings—both revealed and repressed—toward his goricae.

"Aw, look," Caswell complained, "I don't even know what a goricae is."

"Of course you do. You just won't *let* yourself know."

"I don't know. Tell me."

"It would be better if you told me."

"How can I?" Caswell raged. "I don't know!"

"What do you *imagine* a goricae would be?"

"A forest fire," Caswell said. "A salt tablet. A jar of denatured alcohol. A small screwdriver. Am I getting warm? A notebook. A revolver—"

"These associations are meaningful," the Regenerator assured him. "Your attempt at randomness shows a clearly underlying pattern. Do you begin to recognize it?"

"What in hell is a goricae?" Caswell roared.

"The tree that nourished you during infancy, and well into puberty, if my theory about you is correct. Inadvertently, the goricae stifled your necessary rejection of the feem desire. This in turn gave rise to your present urge to dwark someone in a vlendish manner."

"No tree nourished me."

"You cannot recall the experience?"

"Of course not. It never happened."

"You are sure of that?"

"Positive."

"Not even the tiniest bit of doubt?"

"No! No goricae ever nourished me. Look, I can break off these sessions at any time, right?"

"Of course," the Regenerator said. "But it would not be advisable at this moment. You are expressing anger, resentment, fear. By your rigidly summary rejection—"

"Nuts," said Caswell, and pulled off the headband.

The silence was wonderful. Caswell stood up, yawned, stretched and massaged the back of his neck. He stood in front of the humming black machine and gave it a long leer.

"You couldn't cure me of a common cold," he told it.

Stiffly he walked the length of the living room and returned to the Regenerator.

"Lousy fake!" he shouted.

Caswell went into the kitchen and opened a bottle of beer. His revolver was still on the table, gleaming dully.

Magnessen! You unspeakable treacherous filth! You fiend incarnate! You inhuman, hideous monster! Someone must destroy you, Magnessen! Someone . . .

Someone? He himself would have to do it. Only he knew the bottomless depths of Magnessen's depravity, his viciousness, his disgusting lust for power.

Yes, it was his duty, Caswell thought. But strangely, the knowledge brought him no pleasure.

After all, Magnessen was his friend.

He stood up, ready for action. He tucked the revolver into his right-hand coat pocket and glanced at the kitchen clock. Nearly six-thirty. Magnessen would be home now, gulping his dinner, grinning over his plans.

This was the perfect time to take him.

Caswell strode to the door, opened it, started through, and stopped.

A thought had crossed his mind, a thought so tremendously involved, so meaningful, so far-reaching in its implications that he was stirred to his depths. Caswell tried desperately to shake off the knowledge it brought. But the thought, permanently etched upon his memory, would not depart.

Under the circumstances, he could do only one thing.

He returned to the living room, sat down on the couch and slipped on the headband.

The Regenerator said, "Yes?"

"It's the damnedest thing," Caswell said, "but do you know, I think I do remember my goricae!"

"There's no time for explanations," Rath said. "Believe me, it's in his own best interest, too. What is his name?"

Magnessen studied Rath's ugly, honest face, trying to make up his mind.

Lieutenant Smith said, "Come on, talk, Magnessen, if you know what's good for you. We want the name and we want it quick."

It was the wrong approach. Magnessen lighted a cigarette, blew smoke in Smith's direction and inquired, "You got a warrant, buddy?"

"You bet I have," Smith said, striding forward. "I'll warrant you, wise guy."

"Stop it!" Rath ordered. "Lieutenant Smith, thank you for your assistance. I won't need you any longer."

Smith left sulkily, taking his platoon with him.

Rath said, "I apologize for Smith's over-eagerness. You had better hear the problem." Briefly but fully, he told the story of the customer and the Martian therapeutic machine.

When he was finished, Magnessen looked more suspicious than ever. "You say he wants to kill *me?*"

"Definitely."

"That's a lie! I don't know what your game is, mister, but you'll never make me believe that. Elwood's my best friend. We been best friends since we was kids. We been in service together. Elwood would cut off his arm for me. And I'd do the same for him."

"Yes, yes," Rath said impatiently, "in a sane frame of mind, he would. But your friend Elwood—is that his first name or last?"

"First," Magnessen said tauntingly.

"Your friend Elwood is psychotic."

"You don't know him. That guy loves me like a brother. Look, what's Elwood really done? Defaulted on some payments or something? I can help out."

"You thick-headed imbecile!" Rath shouted. "I'm trying to save your life, and the life and sanity of your friend!"

"But how do I know?" Magnessen pleaded. "You guys come busting in here—"

"You must trust me," Rath said.

Magnessen studied Rath's face and nodded sourly. "His name's Elwood Caswell. He lives just down the block at number 341."

The man who came to the door was short, with red hair and red-rimmed eyes. His right hand was thrust into his coat pocket. He seemed very calm.

"Are you Elwood Caswell?" Rath asked. "The Elwood Caswell who bought a Regenerator early this afternoon at the Home Therapy Appliances Store?"

"Yes," said Caswell. "Won't you come in?"

Inside Caswell's small living room, they saw the Regenerator, glistening black and chrome, standing near the couch. It was unplugged.

"Have you used it?" Rath asked anxiously.

"Yes."

Follansby stepped forward. "Mr. Caswell, I don't know how to explain this, but we made a terrible mistake. The Regenerator you took was a Martian model—for giving therapy to Martians."

"I know," said Caswell.

"You do?"

"Of course. It became pretty obvious after a while."

"It was a dangerous situation," Rath said. "Especially for a man with your—ah—troubles." He studied Caswell covertly. The man seemed fine, but appearances were frequently deceiving, especially with psychotics. Caswell had been homicidal; there was no reason why he should not still be.

And Rath began to wish he had not dismissed Smith and his policemen so summarily. Sometimes an armed squad was a comforting thing to have around.

Caswell walked across the room to the therapeutic machine. One hand was still in his jacket pocket; the other he laid affectionately upon the Regenerator.

"The poor thing tried its best," he said. "Of course, it couldn't cure what wasn't there." He laughed. "But it came very near succeeding!"

Rath studied Caswell's face and said, in a trained, casual tone, "Glad there was no harm, sir. The Company will, of course, reimburse you for your lost time and for your mental anguish—"

"Naturally," Caswell said.

"—and we will substitute a proper Terran Regenerator at once."

"That won't be necessary."

"It *won't?*"

"No." Caswell's voice was decisive. "The machine's attempt at therapy forced me into a complete self-appraisal. There was a moment of absolute insight, during which I was able to evaluate and discard my homicidal intentions toward poor Magnessen."

Rath nodded dubiously. "You feel no such urge now?"

"Not in the slightest."

Rath frowned deeply, started to say something, and stopped. He turned to Follansby and Haskins. "Get that machine out of here. I'll have a few things to say to you at the store."

The manager and the clerk lifted the Regenerator and left.

Rath took a deep breath. "Mr. Caswell, I would strongly advise that you accept a new Regenerator from the Company, gratis. Unless a cure effected in a proper mechano-therapeutic manner. there is always the danger of a setback."

"No danger with me," Caswell said, airily but with deep conviction. "Thank you for your consideration, sir. And good night."

Rath shrugged and walked to the door.

"Wait!" Caswell called.

Rath turned. Caswell had taken his hand out of his pocket. In it was a revolver. Rath felt sweat trickle down his arms. He calculated the distance between himself and Caswell. Too far.

"Here," Caswell said, extending the revolver butt-first. "I won't need this any longer."

Rath managed to keep his face expressionless as he accepted the revolver and stuck it into a shapeless pocket.

"Good night," Caswell said. He closed the door behind Rath and bolted it.

At last he was alone.

Caswell walked into the kitchen. He opened a bottle of beer, took a deep swallow and sat down at the kitchen table. He stared fixedly at a point just above and to the left of the clock.

He had to form his plans now. There was no time to lose.

Magnessen! That inhuman monster who cut down the Caswell goricae! Magnessen! The man who, even now, was secretly planning to infect New York with the abhorrent feem desire! Oh, Magnessen, I wish you a long, long life, filled with the torture I can inflict on you. And to start with . . .

Caswell smiled to himself as he planned exactly how he would dwark Magnessen in a vlendish manner.

PROTECTION

There'll be an airplane crash in Burma next week, but it shouldn't affect me here in New York. And the feegs certainly can't harm me. Not with all my closet doors closed.

No, the big problem is lesnerizing. I must not lesnerize. Absolutely not. As you can imagine, that hampers me.

And to top it all, I think I'm catching a really nasty cold.

The whole thing started on the evening of November seventh. I was walking down Broadway on my way to Baker's Cafeteria. On my lips was a faint smile, due to having passed a tough physics exam earlier in the day. In my pocket, jingling faintly, were five coins, three keys and a book of matches.

Just to complete the picture, let me add that the wind was from the northwest at five miles an hour, Venus was in the ascendancy and the Moon was decidedly gibbous. You can draw your own conclusions from this.

I reached the corner of 98th Street and began to cross. As I stepped off the curb, someone yelled at me, "The truck! Watch the truck!"

I jumped back, looking around wildly. There was nothing in sight. Then, a full second later, a truck cut around the corner on two wheels, ran though the red light and roared up Broadway. Without the warning, I would have been hit.

You've heard stories like this, haven't you? About the strange voice that warned Aunt Minnie to stay out of the elevator, which then crashed to the basement. Or maybe it told Uncle Joe not to sail on the *Titanic*. That's where the story usually ends.

I wish mine ended there.

"Thanks, friend," I said and looked around. There was no one there.

"Can you still hear me?" the voice asked.

"Sure I can." I turned a complete circle and stared suspiciously at the closed apartment windows overhead. "But where in the blue blazes are you?"

"Gronish," the voice answered. "Is that the referrent? Refraction index. Creature of insubstantiality. The Shadow knows. Did I pick the right one?"

"You're invisible?" I hazarded.

"That's it!"

"But what are you?"

"A validusian derg."

"A what?"

"I am—open your larynx a little wider please. Let me see now. I am the Spirit of Christmas Past. The Creature from the Black Lagoon. The Bride of Frankenstein. The—"

"Hold on," I said. "What are you trying to tell me—that you're a ghost or a creature from another planet?"

"Same thing," the derg replied. "Obviously."

That made it all perfectly clear. Any fool could see that the voice belonged to someone from another planet. He was invisible on Earth, but his superior senses had spotted an approaching danger and warned me of it.

Just a plain, everyday supernormal incident.

I began to walk hurriedly down Broadway.

"What is the matter?" the invisible derg asked.

"Not a thing," I answered, "except that I seem to be standing in the middle of the street talking to an invisible alien from the farthest reaches of outer space. I suppose only I can hear you?"

"Well, naturally."

"Great! You know where this sort of thing will land me?"

"The concept you are sub-vocalizing is not entirely clear."

"The loony bin. Nut house. Bug factory. Psychotic ward. That's where they put people who talk to invisible aliens. Thanks for the warning, buddy. Good night."

Feeling light-headed, I turned east, hoping my invisible friend would continue down Broadway.

"Won't you talk with me?" the derg asked.

I shook my head, a harmless gesture they can't pick you up for, and kept on walking.

"But you must," the derg said with a hint of desperation. "A real sub-vocal contact is very rare and astonishingly difficult. Sometimes I can get across a warning, just before a danger moment. But then the connection fades."

So there was the explanation for Aunt Minnie's premonition. But I still wasn't having any.

"Conditions might not be right again for a hundred years!" the derg mourned.

What conditions? Five coins and three keys jingling together when Venus was ascendant? I suppose it's worthy of investigation—but not by me. You never can prove that supernormal stuff. There are enough people knitting slipcovers for straitjackets without me swelling their ranks.

"Just leave me alone," I said. A cop gave me a funny look for that one. I grinned boyishly and hurried on.

"I appreciate your social situation," the derg urged, "but this contact is in your own best interests. I want to protect you from the myriad dangers of human existence."

I didn't answer him.

"Well," the derg said, "I can't force you. I'll just have to offer my services elsewhere. Good-by, friend."

I nodded pleasantly.

"One last thing," he said. "Stay off subways tomorrow between noon and one-fifteen P.M. Good-by."

"Huh? Why?"

"Someone will be killed at Columbus Circle, pushed in front of a train by shopping crowds. You, if you are there. Good-by."

"Someone will be killed there tomorrow?" I asked. "You're sure?"

"Of course."

"It'll be in the newspapers?"

"I should imagine so."

"And you know all sorts of stuff like that?"

"I can perceive all dangers radiating toward you and extending into time. My one desire is to protect you from them."

I had stopped. Two girls were giggling at me talking to myself. Now I began walking again.

"Look," I whispered, "can you wait until tomorrow evening?"

"You will let me be your protector?" the derg asked eagerly.

"I'll tell you tomorrow," I said. "After I read the late papers."

The item was there, all right. I read it in my furnished room on 113th street. Man pushed by the crowd, lost his balance, fell in front of an oncoming train. This gave me a lot to think about while waiting for my invisible protector to show up.

I didn't know what to do. His desire to protect me seemed genuine enough. But I didn't know if I wanted it. When, an hour later, the derg contacted me, I liked the whole idea even less, and told him so.

"Don't you trust me?" he asked.

"I just want to lead a normal life."

"If you lead any life at all," he reminded me. "That truck last night—"

"That was a freak, a once-in-a-lifetime hazard."

"It only takes once in a lifetime to die," the derg said solemnly. "There was the subway, too."

"That doesn't count. I hadn't planned on riding it today."

"But you had no reason *not* to ride it. That's the important thing. Just as you have no reason not to take a shower in the next hour."

"Why shouldn't I?"

"A Miss Flynn," the derg said, "who lives down the hall, has just completed her shower and has left a bar of melting pink soap on the pink tile in the bathroom on this floor. You would have slipped on it and suffered a sprained wrist."

"Not fatal, huh?"

"No. Hardly in the same class with, let us say, a heavy flowerpot pushed from a rooftop by a certain unstable old gentleman."

"When is that going to happen?" I asked.

"I thought you weren't interested."

"I'm very interested. When? Where?"

"Will you let me continue to protect you?" he asked.

"Just tell me one thing," I said. "What's in this for you?"

"Satisfaction!" he said. "For a validusian derg, the greatest thrill possible is to aid another creature evade danger."

"But isn't there something else you want out of it? Some trifle like my soul, or rulership of Earth?"

"Nothing! To accept payment for Protecting would ruin the emotional experience. All I want out of life—all any derg wants—is to protect someone from the dangers he cannot see, but which we can see all too well." The derg paused, then added softly, "We don't even expect gratitude."

Well, that clinched it. How could I guess the consequences? How could I know that his aid would lead me into a situation in which I must not lesnerize?

"What about that flowerpot?" I asked.

"It will be dropped on the corner of Tenth Street and McAdams Boulevard at eight-thirty tomorrow morning."

"Tenth and McAdams? Where's that?"

"In Jersey City," he answered promptly.

"But I've never been to Jersey City in my life! Why warn me about that?"

"I don't know where you will or won't go," the derg said. "I merely perceive dangers to you wherever they may occur."

"What should I do now?"

"Anything you wish," he told me. "Just lead your normal life."

Normal life. Hah!

It started out well enough. I attended classes at Columbia, did homework, saw movies, went on dates, played table tennis and chess, all as before. At no time did I let on that I was under the direct protection of a validusian derg.

Once or twice a day, the derg would come to me. He would say something like, "Loose grating on West End Avenue between 66th and 67th Streets. Don't walk on it."

And of course I wouldn't. But someone else would. I often saw these items in the newspapers.

Once I got used to it, it gave me quite a feeling of security. An alien was scurrying around twenty-four hours a day and all he wanted out of life was to protect me. A supernormal bodyguard! The thought gave me an enormous amount of confidence.

My social life, during this period, couldn't have been improved upon.

But the derg soon became overzealous in my behalf. He began finding more and more dangers, most of which had no real bearing on my life in New York—things I should avoid in Mexico City, Toronto, Omaha, Papeete.

I finally asked him if he was planning on reporting every potential danger on Earth.

"These are the few, the very few, that you are or may be affected by," he told me.

"In Mexico City? And Papeete? Why not confine yourself to the local picture? Greater New York, say."

"Locale means nothing to me," the derg replied stubbornly. "My perceptions are temporal, not spatial. I must protect you from *everything!*"

It was rather touching, in a way, and there was nothing I could do about it. I simply had to discard from his reports the various dangers in Hoboken, Thailand, Kansas City, Angkor Vat (collapsing statue), Paris and Sarasota. Then I would reach the local stuff. I would ignore, for the most part, the dangers awaiting me in Queens, the Bronx, Staten Island and Brooklyn, and concentrate on Manhattan.

These were often worth waiting for, however. The derg saved me from some pretty nastly experiences—a holdup on Cathedral Parkway, for example, a teen-age mugging, a fire.

But he kept stepping up the pace. It had started as a report or two a day. Within a month, he was warning me five or six times a day. And at last his warnings, local, national and international, flowed in a continual stream.

I was facing too many dangers, beyond all reasonable probability.

On a typical day:

"Tainted food in Baker's Cafeteria. Don't eat there tonight."

"Amsterdam Bus 312 has bad brakes. Don't ride it."

"Mellen's Tailor Shop has a leaking gas line. Explosion due. Better have your clothes dry-cleaned elsewhere."

"Rabid mongrel on the prowl between Riverside Drive and Central Park West. Take a taxi."

Soon I was spending most of my time not doing things and avoiding places. Danger seemed to be lurking behind every lamp post, waiting for me.

I suspected the derg of padding his report. It seemed the only possible explanation. After all, I had lived this long before meeting him, with no supernormal assistance whatsoever, and had gotten by nicely. Why should the risks increase now?

I asked him that one evening.

"All my reports are perfectly genuine," he said, obviously a little hurt. "If you don't believe me, by turning on the lights in your psychology class tomorrow."

"Why?"

"Defective wiring."

"I don't doubt your warnings," I assured him. "I just know that life was never this dangerous before you came along."

"Of course it wasn't. Surely you know that if you accept protection, you must accept the drawbacks of protection as well."

"Drawbacks like what?"

The derg hesitated. "Protection begets the need of further protection. That is a universal constant."

"Come again?" I asked in bewilderment.

"Before you met me, you were like everyone else and you ran such risks as your situation offered. But with my coming, your immediate environment has changed. And your position in it has changed, too."

"Changed? Why?"

"Because it has me in it. To some extent now, you partake of my environment, just as I partake of yours. And, of course, it is well known that the avoidance of one danger opens the path to others."

"Are you trying to tell me," I said, very slowly, "that my risks have increased because of your help?"

"It was unavoidable," he sighed.

I could have cheerfully strangled the derg at that moment, if he hadn't been invisible and impalpable. I had the angry feeling that I had been conned, taken by an extraterrestrial trickster.

"All right," I said, controlling myself. "Thanks for everything. See you on Mars or wherever you hang out."

"You don't want any further protection?"

"You guessed it. Don't slam the door on your way out."

"But what's wrong?" The derg seemed genuinely puzzled. "There are increased risks in your life, true, but what of it? It is a glory and an honor to face danger and emerge victorious. The greater the peril, the greater the joy of evading it."

For the first time, I saw how alien this alien was.

"Not for me," I said. "Scram."

"Your risks have increased," the derg argued, "but my capacity for detection is more than ample to cope with it. I am happy to cope with it. So it still represents a net gain in protection for you."

I shook my head. "I know what happens next. My risks just keep on increasing, don't they?"

"Not at all. As far as accidents are concerned, you have reached the quantitative limit."

"What does that mean?"

"It means there will be no further increase in the number of accidents you must avoid."

"Good. Now will you please get the hell out of here?"

"But I just explained—"

"Sure, no further increase, just more of the same. Look, if you leave me alone, my original environment will return, won't it? And, with it, my original risks?"

"Eventually," the derg agreed. "If you survive."

"I'll take that chance."

The derg was silent for a time. Finally he said, "You can't afford to send me away. Tomorrow—"

"Don't tell me. I'll avoid the accidents on my own."

"I wasn't thinking of accidents."

"What then?"

"I hardly know how to tell you." He sounded embarrassed. "I said there would be no further quantitative change. But I didn't mention a *qualitative* change."

"What are you talking about?" I shouted at him.

"I'm trying to say," the derg said, "that a gamper is after you."

"A what? What kind of a gag is this?"

"A gamper is a creature from my environment. I suppose he was attracted by your increased potentiality for avoiding risk, due to my protection."

"To hell with the gamper and to hell with you."

"If he comes, try driving him off with mistletoe. Iron is often effective, if bonded to copper. Also—"

I threw myself on the bed and buried my head under the pillow. The derg took the hint. In a moment, I could sense that he was gone.

What an idiot I had been! We denizens of Earth have a common vice: We take what we're offered, whether we need it or not.

You can get into a lot of trouble that way.

But the derg was gone and the worst of my troubles were over. I'd sit tight for a while, give things a chance to work themselves out. In a few weeks, perhaps, I'd . . .

There seemed to be a humming in the air.

I sat upright on the bed. One corner of the room was curiously dark and I could feel a cold breeze on my face. The hum grew louder—not really a hum, but laughter, low and monotonous.

At that point, no one had to draw me a diagram.

"Derg!" I screamed. "Get me out of this!"

He was there. "Mistletoe! Just wave it at the gamper."

"Where in blazes would I get mistletoe?"

"Iron and copper then!"

I leaped to my desk, grabbed a copper paperweight and looked wildly for some iron to bond it to. The paperweight was pulled out of my hand. I caught it before it fell. Then I saw my fountain pen and brought the point against the paperweight.

The darkness vanished. The cold disappeared.

I guess I passed out.

The derg said triumphantly, an hour later, "You see? You need my protection."

"I suppose I do," I answered dully.

"You will need some things," the derg said. "Wolfsbane, amarinth, garlic, graveyard mold—"

"But the gamper is gone."

"Yes. However, the grailers remain. And you need safeguards against the leeps, the feegs and the melgerizer."

So I wrote down his list of herbs, essences and specifics. I didn't bother asking him about this link between supernatural and supernormal. My comprehension was now full and complete.

Ghosts and spirits? Or extraterrestials? All the same, he said, and I saw what he meant. They leave us alone, for the most part. We are on different levels of perception, of existence, even. Until a human is foolish enough to attract attention to himself.

Now I was in their game. Some wanted to kill me, some to protect me, but none cared for me, not even the derg. They were interested solely in my value to the game, if that's what it was.

And the situation was my own fault. At the beginning, I had had the accumulated wisdom of the human race at my disposal, that tremendous racial hatred of witches and ghosts, the irrational fear of alien life. For my adventure has been played out a thousand times and the story is told again and again—how a man dabbles in strange arts and calls to himself a spirit. By so doing, he attracts attention to himself—the worst thing of all.

So I was welded inseparably to the derg and the derg to me. Until yesterday, that is. Now I am on my own again.

Things had been quiet for a few weeks. I had held off the feegs by the simple expedient of keeping my closet doors closed. The leeps were more menacing, but the eye of a toad seemed to stop them. And the melgerizer was dangerous only in the full of the Moon.

"You are in danger," the derg said yesterday.

"Again?" I asked, yawning.

"It is the thrang who pursues us."

"Us?"

"Yes, myself as well as you, for even a derg must run risk and danger."

"Is this thrang particularly dangerous?"

"Very."

"Well, what do I do? Snakeskin over the door? A pentagon?"

"None of those," the derg said. "The thrang must be dealt with negatively, by the avoidance of certain actions."

By now, there were so many restrictions on me, I didn't think another would matter. "What shouldn't I do?"

"You must not lesnerize," the derg said.

"Lesnerize?" I frowned. "What's that?"

"Surely you know. It is a simple, everyday human action."

"I probably know it under a different name. Explain."

"Very well. To lesnerize is to—" He stopped abruptly.

"What?"

"It is here! The thrang!"

I backed up against a wall. I thought I could detect a faint stirring of dust, but that might have been no more than overwrought nerves.

"Derg!" I shouted. "Where are you? What should I do?"

I heard a shriek and the unmistakable sound of jaws snapping.

The derg cried, "It has me!"

"What should I do?" I cried again.

There was a horrible noise of teeth grinding. Very faintly, I heard the derg say, *"Don't lesnerize!"*

And then there was silence.

So I'm sitting tight now. There'll be an airplane crash in Burma next week, but it shouldn't affect me here in New York. And the feegs certainly can't harm me. Not with all my closet doors closed.

No, the problem is lesnerizing. I must *not* lesnerize. Absolutely not. If I can keep from lesnerizing, everything will pass and the chase will move elsewhere. It must! All I have to do is wait them out.

The trouble is, I don't have any idea what lesnerizing might be. A common human action, the derg had said. Well, for the time, I'm avoiding as many actions as possible.

I've caught up on some back sleep and nothing happened, so that's not lesnerizing. I went out and bought food, paid for it, cooked it, ate it. That wasn't lesnerizing. I wrote this report. *That* wasn't lesnerizing.

I'll come out of this yet.

I'm going to catch a nap. I think I have a cold coming on. Now I have to sneez

EARTH, AIR, FIRE
AND WATER

No spaceship radio ever worked properly, and Jim Radell's set on board the *Algonquin* was no exception. He had been talking with Con Electric, back on Earth. But reception faded, and suddenly the tiny pilot's compartment was filled with voices.

"Not grapple *hooks!*" the radio blared. "I wanted candy *bars!*"

"Isn't this Mars Station?" someone asked.

"No, this is Luna. Get the hell off my frequency."

"What am I supposed to do with three gross of grapple hooks?"

"Wear 'em in your nose. Hello, Luna?"

Radell listened for a while. The radio gave him the reassuring impression that space was filled with people, tremendously alive and vital, crowding the planets for room. He had to remind himself that all the noise was made by less than fifty men, specks of dust in the spaces around Earth.

The radio blared static for a few moments, then hummed steadily. Radell switched to standby and strapped himself down. The *Algonquin* was in deceleration orbit, slipping toward the cloudy surface of Venus. He could read a book or take a nap until the ship landed itself.

He had two jobs. One concerned itself with an unmanned ship that Con Electric had sent to Venus five years ago. The ship contained automatic recording instruments. One of Radell's jobs was to return those instruments to Earth.

The *Algonquin* spiraled toward the cold, storm-swept surface of Venus, homing automatically on the grid location of the robot ship. The hull glowed dull red as the *Algonquin* cut through Venus' blanketing atmosphere, slowing, dropping, adjusting itself. Snow flurried around the ship as it turned over, tail jets flaring. Then it settled gently to the ground.

"Sweet landing, baby," Radell told the ship. He unstrapped himself and switched the radio contact to his spacesuit. His dials showed the robot ship two and a half miles away; not

"Would I lie? He broke his arm—"

". . . And four cases of asparagus. Sign my name to it."

"Sure we're in free-fall. He *still* broke his arm."

"This is *Algonquin* calling—"

"Hey, Control, let me in, I'm on the green."

"Priority," Radel called. "Calling Con Electric. I'm stuck in snow. Can't get back to ship. What do I do now?"

The radio blared static.

Radell sat down in the snow to await instructions. He considered the snowfall an imposition. Was he supposed to be an eskimo or something? Con Electric had gotten him into this. Let them get him out.

The suit maintained its even steady warmth. Radell managed to forget his hunger and thirst. As the drifts grew higher, he dozed off.

He awoke in a few hours, thirstier than ever. The radio hummed emptily. Radell realized that he would have to help himself. If he didn't get back to his ship soon, he might become too weak to do anything. The wonderful protective qualities of the suit wouldn't help him then.

He stood up, his throat aching from thirst, and wished that he had packed provisions. But how could he have known he would need them just to walk five miles and wearing such a suit?

He needed a means of locomotion over the thin crust. Snowshoes. What were snowshoes made from on Earth? He knelt and examined one of the thin, pliant plants growing through the snow. This would do as well.

He tried to break one. It was tough and oily. Radell's gloved hands slid right off.

If only he had a knife. But there was no reason for a knife on a spaceship. It was as useless as a spear, or fishhooks.

He tugged again at the plant, then pulled off his gloves and searched his pockets for some sharp instrument. He found nothing except a dog-eared copy of "Planetary Landing Rules for Commercial Ships of More than 500 Gross Tons." He shoved it back in his pocket.

Already his hands were numb. He pushed the gloves back on.

He had an idea. Unzipping the front of his suit, Radell leaned forward and used one side of the zipper as a saw. A cut began to form on the plant, and a blast of wind swept through the opened suit. Radell stepped up the suit's heat output and continued sawing.

By the time he had cut three plants, he found the zipper teeth too dull to use. They should have used a harder alloy, he thought. He opened a zipper in his sleeve and continued sawing.

Finally he had his lengths of plant. He tried to close the zippers, but they were jammed with gum and wood fibers. Radell wrapped the edges as best he could and pushed his heat output to the maximum.

Now to make snowshoes. The plants bent easily, and snapped back easily. He had no way of joining them.

"What a stupid situation," he said out loud. He had no string, no twine, no rope. Nothing.

"What should I do now?" he asked himself.

"Never saw such reception in my life," someone on the radio was saying.

"This is *Algonquin* calling Earth," Radell said hoarsely, for the thousandth time.

"Hello, Mars?"

"Con Electric calling *Algonquin*—"

"Maybe it's the solar corona."

"Cosmic ray output, more likely. Who's that?"

"This is Con Electric. Our ship is delayed—"

"*Algonquin* speaking!" Radell shouted.

"Radell? What are you doing? You're not an explorer and this is no time for sightseeing. Pick up that stuff and get back here."

"This is Luna Station Two—"

"Stay out of this, Luna!" Radell shrieked. "Listen, I'm in a jam. Stuck. Stuck in the snow. Need snowshoes. Snowshoes! Do you hear me?"

The radio growled static. Radell turned back to the problem of snowshoes.

The plants had to be lashed together. The only way Radell could find to do it was by using the wires connecting his radio, or his heating unit. Which should he sacrifice?

It was an uncomfortable choice to make. He needed the radio. But he was cold now, even with the steady work of the heating unit. To destroy that would leave him with just the insulated suit against the cold of Venus.

The radio would have to go, he decided.

". . . Tell her that, will you?" the radio said abruptly. "And on my next leave—" It faded again.

Radell found he couldn't part with the radio, and the voices it brought into the lonely, civilized world of his spacesuit.

Dizzy, tired, his throat parched with thirst, he felt that as long as he could hear the reassuringly mechanical hum of static, he was not alone.

Besides, if the snowshoes didn't work, he would really be stuck without the radio to bring help.

Quickly, before he could change his mind, he ripped out the heating unit, stripped off his gloves, and went to work.

It wasn't as simple as he had thought. He could hardly see, for his plastic helmet fogged with steam, now that the defroster was out of order. The knots he tied in the slippery, plastic-insulated wire pulled out. He tied more complicated knots, and still they pulled out. By trial and error he found one that would hold.

And even then, the plants slipped through the bindings. He had to rough them against the zippers before they would grip.

With one snowshoe partially finished, a wave of dizziness made him stop. He had to have something to drink.

He stripped off his helmet and stuffed a handful of snow into his mouth. It eased his thirst somewhat.

With the helmet off, he could see better. His fingers and toes were dead, and numbness was creeping through his limbs.

It didn't hurt. As a matter of fact, it was quite comfortable. He was very sleepy, he found. Never had he been so sleepy.

He decided to take a very short nap, and then begin again.

"Emergency priority. Emergency priority, Con Electric, calling *Algonquin*. Come in, *Algonquin*. What's wrong *Algonquin?*"

"Snowshoes. Can't get to ship," Radell muttered, half asleep.

"What happened, Radell? Mechanical breakdown? Something wrong with the ship?"

"Ship's all right."

"The suit! Did the suit break down?"

"No—" Radell was very drowsy. He didn't know how to explain what had happened, because he wasn't sure himself. Somehow, he had been taken out of civilization and plunged back a million years, to a time when men lived against the elements. Only a little while ago he had been encased in steel, and fires had spurted at his fingertips. Now he lay against the earth, and his battle was with the forces of fire, air and water.

"Can't explain. Just get me out of here," Radell said.

It suddenly struck him that in all the time of mankind, nothing had changed. Perhaps the cave was a little bigger, the flints a little better, but man himself was no bigger, no tougher, no better fit. Outside, the storm still raged, the elements were supreme.

He shook himself fully awake and staggered to his feet, sure that he had made an important discovery. For the first time, he understood that he was fighting for his life, exactly as billions of his race had fought since the dawn of time, and as they would fight, no matter how well they build their spaceships.

He wasn't going to die. Not easily, anyhow.

He had to have a fire, at once. There was a book of matches in his pants pocket.

Quickly he stripped off his spacesuit to get at them, and stood in the snow in pants and shirt. Next, he built a windbreak out of snow, scooping a hole down to the ground. He arranged branches carefully, and added leaves from the dog-eared "Planetary Landing Rules." He touched a match to it.

If it didn't burn—

But it did burn! The oil in the branches caught at once, and they blazed up, melting the snow around them.

Radell filled his plastic helmet with snow and placed it near the fire. He would have some water now!

He hugged himself close to the blazing branches, scorching his shirt. Already the fire was burning low. He added all the branches he had left.

They weren't enough. Even with the half-finished snowshoe, his fire could last only a little while.

"Do you know what she said to me? Do you really want to know what she said to me? She said—"

"Priority! Emergency priority. Get off the air, everybody. Listen, Radell, this is Con Electric. A ship is putting out from Luna for you. Can you hear me?"

"I can hear you. How soon will it be here?" Radell asked.

"Can't you hear us, Radell? Are you all right? Answer if you can."

"I can hear you. How soon will the ship—"

"You're not coming through. Anyhow, we're assuming that you're still alive. The ship will be there in about ten hours. Hang on, Radell."

Ten hours! His fire was almost gone. Furiously, Radell sawed off more plants. But he couldn't gather them fast enough to keep the fire going.

His water was melted. He gulped it down and burrowed

lower, as close to the earth as he could get. He wrapped the suit around him and leaned close to the fading fire.

Ten hours!

He wanted to tell them that the spacesuit was fine. The only trouble was, Venus had pulled him out of it.

The wind roared over his head, deflected by the windbreak. The fire died to a tiny flame. Radell looked wildly around the white landscape, looking for something, anything to burn.

"Hang on, fella. We're coming down. Made it in seven and a half hours. Burnt up all our fuel. They'll have to send a fuel ship out to us. But we got here."

A bright flame blossomed in Venus' gray sky, and sank toward the silent hulk of the *Algonquin.*

"Can you hear us, boy? Are you still alive? We're almost down."

The ship landed on its tail within a hundred yards of the *Algonquin.* Three men climbed out, into the deep snow. A fourth man brought down several pairs of snowshoes.

"He was sure right about those snowshoes, you know?"

They grouped together and examined a dial on one man's wrist.

"His radio's still on. This way!"

They pushed over the snow, stumbling over each other in their haste. After a mile they were moving slower, but still homing steadily toward the radio signal.

They found Radell crouched over a small fire. His radio lay a few yards from him, where, apparently, he had turned it. He looked up as the men approached and tried to grin.

They saw his spacesuit on the ground, ripped open. Radell was feeding his fire with chunks of lining from the best and most expensive spacesuit man had ever devised.

DEADHEAD

I drove down to Marsport a few hours after the Earth ship landed. There were diamond-tip drills on board, which I had had on requisition for over a year. I wanted to claim them before someone took them. That's not to imply that anyone would *steal* anything; we're all gentlemen and scientists here on Mars. But things are hard to get, and theft-by-priority is the way a gentleman-scientist steals what he needs.

I loaded my drills into the jeep just as Carson from Mining drove up waving a Most Urgent Top Crash Priority. Luckily, I had had the good sense to secure a topmost priority from Director Burke. Carson was so pleasant about it that I gave him three drills.

He chugged away on his scooter, over the red sands of Mars that look so good in color photography, but gum up engines so completely.

I walked over to the Earth ship, not because I give a damn about spaceships, but just to look at something different.

Then I saw the deadhead.

He was standing near the spaceship, his eyes as big as saucers, looking at the red sand, the scorched landing pits, the five buildings of Marsport. The expression on his face said, "Mars! Gee!"

I groaned inwardly. I had more work that day than I could accomplish in a month. But the deadhead was my problem. Director Burke, in a moment of unusual whimsy, had said to me, "Tully, you have a way with people. You understand them. They like you. Therefore I am appointing you Mars Security Chief."

Which meant I was in charge of deadheads.

This particular one was about twenty years old. He was over six feet tall, with perhaps a hundred some very odd pounds of ill-nourished meat on his bones. His nose was turning a bright red in our healthy Martian climate. He had big, clumsy-looking hands, big feet, and he was gasping like a fish out of water in our healthy Martian atmosphere. Naturally, he didn't have a respirator. Deadheads never do.

I walked up to him and said, "Well, how do you like it here?"

"Gol-lee!" he said.

"Quite a feeling, isn't it?" I asked him. "Actually standing on a real honest-to-John alien planet."

"I'll say it is!" the deadhead gasped. He was turning a faint blue from oxygen starvation, all except the tip of his nose. I decided to let him suffer a little longer.

"So you stowed away on that freighter," I said. "You rode deadhead to wonderful, enchanting, exotic Mars."

"Well, I don't think you could call me a stowaway," he said, fighting for breath. "I sorta—sorta—"

"Sorta bribed the captain," I finished for him. By this time, he was weaving unsteadily on his long, skinny legs. I pulled out my spare respirator and clapped it over his nose.

"Come on, deadhead," I said. "I'll get you something to eat. Then you and I are going to have a serious talk."

I held his arm on the way to the mess hall, because he was goggling so hard he would have fallen over something and broken it. Inside, I boosted the atmosphere and warmed some pork and beans for him.

He wolfed them down, leaned back in the chair and grinned ear from ear. "My name's Johnny Franklin," he said. "Mars! I can't believe I'm really here."

That's what all the deadheads say, those who survive the trip. There are about ten attempts a year, but only one or two make it alive. They're such idiots, most of them. A deadhead manages to sneak on board a freighter, in spite of all the security checks.

The ship takes off at about twenty Gs and, without special protection, the deadhead is crushed flat. If he survives that, radiation gets him. Or he's asphyxiated in the airless hold, before he can reach the pilot's compartment.

We've got a special graveyard here, just for deadheads.

But a few of them pull through, and they walk onto Mars with big hopes and stars in their eyes.

I'm the guy who has to disillusion them.

"Just what did you come to Mars for?" I asked.

"I'll tell you," Franklin said. "On Earth you gotta do just like everybody else does. You gotta think like everybody else and act like everybody else or they lock you up."

I nodded. Earth was stable now, for the first time in the

history of mankind. World peace, world government, world prosperity. The authorities wanted to keep it that way. I think they go too far in the suppression of even harmless individualism, but who am I to say? Things will probably relax in a hundred years or so, but that's not good enough for a deadhead living now.

"So you felt the need of new horizons," I said.

"Yes, sir," Franklin said. "I hope this doesn't sound too corny to you, sir, but I want to be a pioneer. I don't care how hard it is. I'll work! You'll see, just let me stay, please, sir! I'll work so hard—"

"Doing what?" I asked.

"Huh?" He looked startled for a moment. Then he said, "I'll do anything."

"But what can you do? We could use a good inorganic chemist, of course. Do your skills happen to run along that line?"

"No, sir," the deadhead said.

I didn't enjoy doing this, but it was important to impress the grim and unpalatable truth upon deadheads. "So your field isn't chemistry," I mused. "Might have a spot for a topnotch geologist. Or possibly a statistician."

"I'm afraid—"

"Tell me, Franklin, have you got your Ph.D.?"

"No, sir."

"Doctorate? Masters? Have you even got a B.S.?"

"No, sir," Franklin said miserably. "I never even finished high school."

"Then just what do you think you can do here?" I asked.

"Well, sir," Franklin said. "I read where the Project is scattered all over Mars. I thought I could be maybe a messenger, sorta. And I can also do carpentry, and some plumbing and—there must be something I can do here."

I poured Franklin another cup of coffee and he looked at me, his big eyes pleading. The deadheads always look like that when we reach this point. They think that Mars is like Alaska in the '70s, or Antarctica in 2000; a frontier for brave, determined men. But Mars isn't a frontier. It's a dead end.

"Franklin," I said, "did you know that Mars Project is not self-supporting, and may never be? Did you know that it costs the project about fifty thousand dollars a year to maintain a man here? Do you figure you're worth a salary of fifty thousand a year?"

"I won't eat much," Franklin said. "And once I get the hang of things I'll—"

"And," I broke in, "were you also aware that there isn't a man on Mars who doesn't hold at least the title of Doctor?"

"I didn't know that," Franklin whispered.

Deadheads never do. I have to tell them. So I told Franklin that scientists do the plumbing, carpentry, messenger work, the cooking, cleaning and repairing, all in their spare time. Not well, perhaps, but it gets done.

The fact is: There is no unskilled labor on Mars. We just can't afford it.

I thought he'd burst into tears, but he managed to control himself.

He stared wistfully around the room, looking at everything in our crummy little mess hall. You see, it was all Martian.

"Come on," I said, standing up. "I'll find a bed for you. Tomorrow we'll arrange your passage back to Earth. Don't feel so bad. At least you've seen Mars."

"Yes, sir." The deadhead stood up wearily. "But, sir, I am not going back to Earth."

I didn't argue with him. A lot of deadheads talk big. How was I to know what this one had in his mind?

After settling Franklin, I returned to my lab and did a few hours work that absolutely had to be done. Then I fell into bed exhausted.

The next morning, I went to wake Franklin. He wasn't in his bed. Immediately I thought of the possibility of sabotage. Who knows what a thwarted pioneer will do? Pull some rods out of the pile, perhaps, or set off the fuel dump. I scurried around the camp looking frantically, and finally found him at the half-built spec lab.

The spec lab was necessarily a spare-time project with us. Whenever anyone had an extra half hour, he mortared a few bricks, sawed out a table-top, or screwed hinges on a door. No one could be spared from his work long enough to really put the thing together.

Franklin had accomplished more in a few hours than most of us had in a few months. He was a good carpenter, all right, and he worked as though all the furies of hell were pursuing him.

"Franklin!" I shouted.

"Yes, sir." He hurried over to me. "Just wanted to do something for my keep, Mr. Tully. Give me a few more hours and I'll have a roof on her. And if no one's using those pipe lengths over there, I could maybe finish the plumbing by tomorrow."

Franklin was a good man, all right. He was just the sort Mars needed. By all the rules of human decency and justice I should have patted him on the shoulder and said, "Boy, book-learning isn't everything. You can stay. We need you."

I really wanted to say just that. But I couldn't. There are no success stories on Mars. No deadhead makes good. We scientists can manage the carpentry and plumbing, poor though the results may be. And we just can't afford duplication of skills.

"Will you please stop making this hard for me, Franklin? I'm a soft-hearted slob. You've convinced me. But all I can do is enforce the rules. You must go back."

"I can't go back," Franklin said very softly.

"Huh?"

"They'll lock me up if I go back," Franklin said.

"All right, tell me about it," I groaned. "But please make it quick."

"Yes, sir. Like I told you," Franklin said. "On Earth, you gotta do like everybody else, and think like everybody else. Well, that was fine for a while. But then I discovered The Truth."

"You what?"

"I discovered The Truth," Franklin said proudly. "I found it by accident, but it was really very simple. It was so simple, I taught it to my sister, and if she could learn it, anyone could. Then I tried to teach it to everybody."

"Go on," I said.

"Well, everybody got very angry. They told me I was crazy, I should shut up. But I couldn't shut up, Mr. Tully, because it was The Truth. So when they went to lock me up, I came to Mars."

Oh, great, I thought. Franklin was just what we needed on Mars. A good, old-fashioned religious fanatic to preach to us hardened scientists. And he was just what the doctor ordered for me. Now, after sending him back to Earth—to prison— I could suffer guilt feelings the rest of my life.

"And that isn't all," Franklin said.

"You mean there's more to this pathetic tale?"

"Yes, sir."

"Go on," I said with a sigh.

"They're after my sister, too," Franklin said. "You see, after she saw The Truth, she was as eager to teach it as me. It's The Truth, you know. So now she has to hide, until— until—" He wiped his nose and gulped miserably. "I thought

I could show you how good I'd be on Mars, and then my sister could join me and—"

"Stop!" I said.

"Yes, sir."

"I don't want to hear any more," I told him. "I've already listened to you too much."

"Would you like me to tell you The Truth?" Franklin asked eagerly. "I could explain—"

"Not another word," I barked.

"Yes, sir."

"Franklin, there is nothing, absolutely nothing I can do for you. You haven't got the qualifications. I haven't the authority to allow you to stay. But I will do the only thing I can do. I'll speak to the Director about you."

"Gee! Thanks a lot, Mr. Tully. Would you explain to him that I haven't really recovered from that trip yet? Once I get my strength back, I'll show you—"

"Sure, sure," I said, and hurried off.

The Director stared at me as though I had slipped my regulator. "But Tully," he said, "you know the rules."

"Sure," I said. "But he really would be useful. And I hate to ship him back to the police."

"It costs fifty thousand dollars a year to maintain a man on Mars," the Director said. "Do you think he's worth a salary of—"

"I know, I know," I said. "But he's such a pathetic case, and he's so eager, and we could use—"

"All deadheads are pathetic," the Director said.

"Yeah. After all, they're inferior human beings, not like us scientists. So back he goes."

"Ed," the Director spoke quietly. "I can see resentment building between us over this. Therefore I'm going to leave it up to you. You know that there are close to ten thousand applications a year for a berth in Mars Project. We turn back better men than ourselves. Kids in the universities study for years to fill a specific place here, and then find the position already taken. Considering all that, do you honestly feel that Franklin should stay?"

"I—I—oh, damnit, no, if you put it that way." I was still angry.

"Is there any other way to put it?" the Director asked.

"Of course not."

"It's a sad situation when many are called but few are chosen," the Director mused. "There's a need for a new frontier. I'd like to open Mars wide open for colonization. And someday we will. But not until we're self-supporting."

"Right," I said. "I'll arrange for the deadhead's return."

Franklin was working on the roof of the spec lab when I returned, and he had only to look at my face to know what the answer was.

I climbed in my jeep and drove to Marsport. I had quite a few harsh words to say to the captain of the space freighter who had allowed Franklin on board. Too much of that stuff goes on. This joker was going to carry Franklin back to Earth.

The freighter was in the blast pit, its nose pointing skyward. Clarkson, our atomics man, was readying it for takeoff.

"Where's the captain of this heap?" I asked.

"No captain," Clarkson said. "This is a drone model. Radio-controlled."

My stomach started to do slow flip-flops. "No captain?"

"Nope."

"Any crew?"

"Not on a drone," Clarkson said. "You know that, Tully."

"In that case," I said brightly, "there's no oxygen on board."

"Of course not!"

"And no radiation shielding."

"That's right." Clarkson stared at me.

"And no insulation."

"Just enough to keep the hull from melting."

"I suppose it took off at top acceleration. Thirty-five or so Gs."

"Sure," Clarkson said. "That's the economical way, if you haven't got humans on board. What's eating you?"

I didn't answer him. I just walked to the jeep and roared back to the spec lab. My stomach was no longer doing flip-flops. It was spinning like a top.

A human couldn't have lived through that trip. Not a chance. Not a chance in ten billion. It was a physical impossibility.

When I reached the lab, Franklin had completed the roof and was on the ground, connecting pipes. It was lunchtime, and several of the men from Mining were helping him.

"Franklin," I said.

"Yes, sir?"

I took a deep breath. "Franklin, did you come here on that freighter?"

"No, sir," he said. "I tried to tell you that I didn't bribe no captain, but you wouldn't—"

"In that case," I spoke very slowly, "how did you get here?"

"By using The Truth!"

"Could you show me?"

Franklin considered for a moment. "The trip tired me out something awful, Mr. Tully," he said, "but I guess I could."

And he disappeared.

I stood there, blinking. Then one of the Mining men pointed overhead. There was Franklin, hovering at about three hundred feet.

In another moment, he was standing beside me again, his nose pinched and red from the cold.

It looked like instantaneous transfer. Oh, brother.

"Is that The Truth?" I asked.

"Yes, sir," Franklin said. "It's a different way of looking at things. Once you see it—*really* see it—you can do all sorts of things. But they called it a—a hallucination on Earth, and they said I had to stop hypnotizing people and—"

"You can teach this?" I asked.

"Sure," Franklin said. "It may take a little time, though."

"That's all right. I guess we can afford a little time. Yessiree, I guess we sure can. Yessiree, a little time spent on The Truth might be well spent—"

I don't know how much longer I would have gone on babbling, but Franklin broke in eagerly.

"Mr. Tully, does that mean I can stay?"

"You can stay, Franklin. As a matter of fact, if you try to leave, I'll shoot you."

"Oh, thank you, sir! And how about my sister? Can she come?"

"Oh, yes, most certainly," I said. "Your sister can come. Any time she—"

I heard a startled shriek from the Mining men. The hairs on the back of my neck stood on end, and I turned very slowly.

There stood a girl, a tall, skinny girl with eyes as big as saucers. She stared around like a sleepwalker and murmured, "Mars! Gol-*lee!*"

Then she turned to me and blushed.

"I'm sorry, sir," she said. "I—I was listening in."

THE ACADEMY

INSTRUCTION SHEET FOR USE WITH THE CA-HILL-THOMAS SANITY METER, SERIES JM-14 (MANUAL):

The Cahill-Thomas Manufacturing Company is pleased to present our newest Sanity Meter. This beautiful, rugged instrument, small enough for any bedroom, kitchen or den, is in all respects an exact replica of the larger C-T Sanity Meters used in most places of business, recreation, transportation, etc. No pains have been spared to give you the best Sanity Meter possible, at the lowest possible price.

1. OPERATION. At the lower right-hand corner of your Meter is a switch. Turn it to On position, and allow a few seconds for warming up. Then switch from On position to Operate position. Allow a few seconds for reading.

2. READING. On the front of your Meter, above the operating switch, is a transparent panel, showing a straight-line scale numbered from zero to ten. The number at which the black indicator stops shows your Sanity Reading, in relation to the present statistical norm.

3. EXPLANATION OF NUMBERS ZERO TO THREE. On this model, as on all Sanity Meters, zero is the theoretically perfect sanity point. Everything above zero is regarded as a deviation from the norm. However, zero is a statistical rather than an actual idea. The normalcy range for our civilization lies between zero and three. Any rating in this area is considered normal.

4. EXPLANATION OF NUMBERS FOUR TO SEVEN. These numbers represent the sanity-tolerance limit. Persons registering in this area should consult their favorite therapy at once.

5. EXPLANATION OF NUMBERS EIGHT TO TEN. A person who registers above seven is considered a highly dangerous potential to his milieu. Almost certainly he is highly neurotic, prepsychotic or psychotic. This individual is *required by law* to register his rating, and to bring it below seven within a probationary period. (Consult your state laws for periods of

probation.) Failing this, he must undergo Surgical Alteration, or may submit voluntarily to therapy at The Academy.

6. EXPLANATION OF NUMBER TEN. At ten on your Meter there is a red line. If a sanity-reading passes this line, the individual so registered can no longer avail himself of the regular commercial therapies. This individual must undergo Surgical Alteration immediately, or submit at once to therapy at The Academy.

WARNING:

A. THIS IS NOT A DIAGNOSTIC MACHINE. DO NOT ATTEMPT TO DETERMINE FOR YOURSELF WHAT YOUR AILMENT IS. THE NUMBERS ZERO TO TEN REPRESENT INTENSITY QUALITIES, NOT ARBITRARY CLASSIFICATIONS OF NEUROTIC, PREPSYCHOTIC, PSYCHOTIC, ETC. THE INTENSITY SCALE IS IN REFERENCE ONLY TO AN INDIVIDUAL'S POTENTIAL FOR HARM TO HIS SOCIAL ORDER. A PARTICULAR TYPE OF NEUROTIC MAY BE POTENTIALLY MORE DANGEROUS THAN A PSYCHOTIC, AND WILL SO REGISTER ON ANY SANITY METER. SEE A THERAPIST FOR FURTHER INSIGHT.

B. THE ZERO-TO-TEN READINGS ARE APPROXIMATE. FOR AN EXACT THIRTY DECIMAL RATING, GO TO A COMMERCIAL MODEL C-T METER.

C. REMEMBER—SANITY IS EVERYONE'S BUSINESS. WE HAVE COME A LONG WAY SINCE THE GREAT WORLD WARS, ENTIRELY BECAUSE WE HAVE FOUNDED OUR CIVILIZATION ON THE CONCEPTS OF SOCIAL SANITY, INDIVIDUAL RESPONSIBILITY, AND PRESERVATION OF THE STATUS QUO. THEREFORE, IF YOU RATE OVER THREE, GET HELP. IF YOU RATE OVER SEVEN, YOU MUST GET HELP. IF YOU RATE OVER TEN, DO NOT WAIT FOR DETECTION AND ARREST. GIVE YOURSELF UP VOLUNTARILY IN THE NAME OF CIVILIZATION.

Good Luck—
The Cahill-Thomas Company

After finishing his breakfast, Mr. Feerman knew he should leave immediately for work. Under the circumstances, any tardiness might be construed unfavorably He went so far as to put on his neat gray hat, adjust his tie and start for the door. But, his hand on the knob, he decided to wait for the mail.

He turned away from the door, annoyed with himself, and began to pace up and down the living room. He had known he was going to wait for the mail; why had he gone through the pretense of leaving? Couldn't he be honest with himself, even now, when personal honesty was so important?

His black cocker spaniel Speed, curled up on the couch, looked curiously at him. Feerman patted the dog's head, reached for a cigarette, and changed his mind. He patted Speed again, and the dog yawned lazily. Feerman adjusted a lamp that needed no adjusting, shuddered for no reason, and began to pace the room again.

Reluctantly, he admitted to himself that he didn't want to leave his apartment, dreaded it in fact, although nothing was going to happen. He tried to convince himself that this was just another day, like yesterday and the day before. Certainly if a man could believe that, really believe it, events would defer indefinitely, and nothing would happen to him.

Besides, why should anything happen today? He wasn't at the end of his probationary period yet.

He thought he heard a noise outside his apartment, hurried over and opened the door. He had been mistaken; the mail hadn't arrived. But down the hall his landlady opened her door and looked at him with pale, unfriendly eyes.

Feerman closed the door and found that his hands were shaking. He decided that he had better take a sanity reading. He entered the bedroom, but his robutler was there, sweeping a little pile of dust toward the center of the room. Already his bed was made; his wife's bed didn't require making, since it had been unoccupied for almost a week.

"Shall I leave, sir?" the robutler asked.

Feerman hesitated before answering. He preferred taking his reading alone. Of course, his robutler wasn't really a person. Strictly speaking, the mechanical had no personality; but he had what seemed like a personality. Anyhow, it didn't matter whether he stayed or left, since all personal robots had sanity-reading equipment built into their circuits. It was required by law.

"Suit yourself," he said finally.

The robutler sucked up the little pile of dust and rolled noiselessly out of the room.

Feerman stepped up to the Sanity Meter, turned it on and set the operating control. He watched morosely as the black indicator climbed slowly through the normal twos and threes, through the deviant sixes and sevens, and rested finally on eight-point-two.

One tenth of a point higher than yesterday. One tenth closer to the red line.

Feerman snapped off the machine and lighted a cigarette.

He left the bedroom slowly, wearily, as though the day were over, instead of just beginning.

"The mail, sir," the robutler said, gliding up to him. Feerman grabbed the letters from the robutler's outstretched hand and looked through them.

"She didn't write," he said involuntarily.

"I'm sorry, sir," the robutler responded promptly.

"You're sorry?" Feerman looked at the mechanical curiously. "Why?"

"I am naturally interested in your welfare, sir," the robutler stated. "As is Speed, to the extent of his intelligence. A letter from Mrs. Feerman would have helped your morale. We are sorry it didn't come."

Speed barked softly and cocked his head to one side. Sympathy from a machine, Feerman thought, pity from a beast. But he was grateful all the same.

"I don't blame her," he said. "She couldn't be expected to put up with me forever." He waited, hoping that the robot would tell him that his wife would return, that he would soon be well. But the robutler stood silently beside Speed, who had gone to sleep again.

Feerman looked through the mail again. There were several bills, an advertisement, and a small, stiff letter. The return address on it was The Academy, and Feerman opened it quickly.

Within was a card, which read, "Dear Mr. Feerman, your application for admission has been processed and found acceptable. We will be happy to receive you at any time. Thank You, the Directors."

Feerman squinted at the card. He had never applied for admission to The Academy. It was the last thing in the world he wanted to do. "Was this my wife's idea?" he asked.

"I do not know, sir," the robutler said.

Feerman turned the card over in his hand. He had always been vaguely aware of the existence of The Academy, of course. One couldn't help but be aware of it, since its presence affected every strata of life. But actually, he knew very little about this important institution, surprisingly little.

"What is The Academy?" he asked.

"A large low gray building," his robutler answered. "It is situated in the Southwest corner of the city, and can be reached by a variety of public conveyances."

"But what is it?"

"A registered therapy," the robutler said, "open to anyone upon application, written or verbal. Moreover, The Academy exists as a voluntary choice for all people of plus ten rating, as an alternative to Surgical Personality Alteration."

Feerman sighed with exasperation "I know all that. But what is their system? What kind of therapy?"

"I do not know, sir," the robutler said.

"What's their record of cures?"

"One hundred percent," the robutler answered promptly.

Feerman remembered something else now, something that struck him as rather strange. "Let me see," he said. "No one leaves The Academy. Is that right?"

"There has been no record of anyone leaving after physically entering," the robutler said.

"Why?"

"I do not know, sir."

Feerman crumpled the card and dropped it into an ashtray. It was all very strange. The Academy was so well known, so accepted, one never thought to ask about it. It had always been a misty place in his mind, far-away, unreal. It was the place you went to if you became plus ten, since you didn't want to undergo lobotomy, topectomy, or any other process involving organic personality loss. But of course you tried not to think of the possibility of becoming plus ten, since the very thought was an admission of instability, and therefore you didn't think of the choices open to you if it happened.

For the first time in his life, Feerman decided he didn't like the setup. He would have to do some investigating. Why didn't anyone leave The Academy? Why wasn't more known of their therapy, if their cures were really one hundred percent effective?

"I'd better get to work," Feerman said. "Make me anything at all for supper."

"Yes, sir. Have a good day, sir."

Speed jumped down from the couch and followed him to the door. Feerman knelt down and stroked the dog's sleek black head. "No, boy, you stay inside. No burying bones today."

"Speed does not bury bones," the robutler said.

"That's right." Dogs today, like their masters, rarely had a feeling of insecurity. No one buried bones today. "So long." He hurried past his landlady's door and into the street.

Feerman was almost twenty minutes late for work. As he

entered the building, he forgot to present his probationary certificate to the scanning mechanism at the door. The gigantic commercial Sanity Meter scanned him, its indicator shot past the seven point, lights flashed red. A harsh metallic voice shouted over the loudspeaker, "Sir! Sir! Your deviation from the norm has passed the safety limit! Please arrange for therapy at once!"

Quickly Feerman pulled his probationary certificate out of his wallet. But perversely, the machine continued to bellow at him for a full ten seconds longer. Everyone in the lobby was staring at him. Messenger boys stopped dead, pleased at having witnessed a disturbance. Businessmen and office girls whispered together, and two Sanity Policemen exchanged meaningful glances. Feerman's shirt, soaked with perspiration, was plastered against his back. He resisted an urge to run from the building, instead walked toward an elevator. But it was nearly full, and he couldn't bring himself to enter.

He trotted up a staircase to the second floor, and then took an elevator the rest of the way up. By the time he reached the Morgan Agency he had himself under control. He showed his probationary certificate to the Sanity Meter at the door, mopped his face with a handkerchief, and walked in.

Everyone in the agency knew what had happened. He could tell by their silence, their averted faces. Feerman walked rapidly to his office, closed the door and hung up his hat.

He sat down at his desk, still slightly out of wind, filled with resentment at the Sanity Meter. If only he could smash all the damned things! Always prying, setting off their alarms in your ear, unstabilizing you . . .

Feerman cut off the thought quickly. There was nothing wrong with the Meters. To think of them as active persecuting agents was paranoidal, and perhaps a symptom of his present unsane status. The Meters were mere extensions of man's will. Society as a whole, he reminded himself, must be protected against the individual, just as a human body must be protected against malfunction of any of its parts. As fond as you might be of your gall bladder, you would sacrifice it mercilessly if it were going to impair the rest of you.

He sensed something shaky in this analogy, but decided not to pursue it any farther. He had to find out more about The Academy.

After lighting a cigarette he dialed the Therapy Reference Service.

"May I help you, sir?" a pleasant-voiced woman answered.

"I'd like to get some information about The Academy," Feerman said, feeling a trifle foolish. The Academy was so well known, so much a part of everyday life, it was tantamount to asking what form of government your country had.

"The Academy is located—"

"I know where it's located," Feerman said. "I want to know what sort of therapy they administer."

"That information is not available, sir," the woman said, after a pause.

"No? I thought all data on commercial therapies was available to the public."

"Technically, it is," the woman answered slowly. "But The Academy is not, strictly, a commercial therapy. It does accept money; however, it admits charity cases as well, without quota. Also, it is partially supported by the government."

Feerman tapped the ash off his cigarette and said impatiently, "I thought all government projects were open to the public."

"As a general rule, they are. Except when such knowledge will be harmful to the public."

"Then such knowledge of The Academy *would* be harmful?" Feerman said triumphantly, feeling that he was getting to the heart of the matter.

"Oh, no sir!" The woman's voice became shrill with amazement. "I didn't mean to imply that! I was just stating the general rules for withholding of information. The Academy, although covered by the laws, is, to some extent, extra-legal. This status is allowed because of The Academy's one-hundred percent record of cures."

"Where can I see a few of these cures?" Feerman asked. "I understand that no one ever leaves The Academy."

He had them now, Feerman thought, waiting for an answer. Over the telephone he thought he heard a whispering. Suddenly a man's voice broke in, loud and clear. "This is the Section Chief. Is there some difficulty?"

Hearing the man's sharp voice, Feerman almost dropped the telephone. His feeling of triumph vanished, and he wished he had never made the call. But he forced himself to go on. "I want some information on The Academy."

"The location—"

"No! I mean real information!" Feerman said desperately.

"To what purpose do you wish to put this information?" the Section Chief asked, and his voice was suddenly the smooth, almost hypnotic voice of a therapist.

"Insight," Feerman answered quickly. "Since The Academy is a therapeutic alternative open to me at all times, I would like to know more about it, in order to judge—"

"Very plausible," the Section Chief said. "But consider. Are you asking for a useful, functional insight? One that will better your integration into society? Or are you asking merely for the sake of an overriding curiosity, thereby yielding to restlessness, and other, deeper drives?"

"I'm asking because—"

"What is your name?" the Section Chief asked suddenly. Feerman was silent.

"What is your sanity rating?"

Still Feerman didn't speak. He was trying to decide if the call were already traced, and decided that it was.

"Do you doubt The Academy's essential benevolence?"

"No."

"Do you doubt that The Academy works for the preservation of the Status Quo?"

"No."

"Then what is your problem? Why won't you tell me your name and sanity rating? Why do you feel this need for more information?"

"Thank you," Feerman murmured, and hung up. He realized that the telephone call had been a terrible mistake. It had been the action of a plus-eight, not a normal man. The Section Chief, with his trained perceptions, had realized that at once. Of course the Section Chief wouldn't give information to a plus-eight! Feerman knew he would have to watch his actions far more closely, analyze them, understand them, if he ever hoped to return to the statistical norm.

As he sat, there was a knock; the door opened and his boss, Mr. Morgan entered. Morgan was a big, powerfully built man with a full, fleshy face. He stood in front of Feerman's desk, drumming his fingers on the blotter, looking as embarrassed as a caught thief.

"Heard that report downstairs," he said, not looking at Feerman, tapping his fingers energetically.

"Momentary peak," Feerman said automatically. "Actually, my rating has begun to come down." He couldn't look at Morgan as he said this. The two men stared intently at different corners of the room. Finally, their eyes met.

"Look, Feerman, I try to stay out of people's business," Morgan said, sitting on the corner of Feerman's desk. "But damn it, man, Sanity is everyone's business. We're all in the game together." The thought seemed to increase Morgan's conviction. He leaned forward earnestly.

"You know, I'm responsible for a lot of people here. This is the third time in a year you've been on probation." He hesitated. "How did it start?"

Feerman shook his head. "I don't know, Mr. Morgan. I was just going along quietly—and my rating started to climb."

Morgan considered, then shook his head. "Can't be as simple as that. Have you been checked for brain lesions?"

"I've been assured it's nothing organic."

"Therapy?"

"Everything," Feerman said. "Electro-therapy, Analysis, Smith's Method, The Rannes School, Devio-Thought, Differentiation—"

"What did they say?" Morgan asked.

Feerman thought back on the endless line of therapists he had gone to. He had been explored from every angle that psychology had to offer. He had been drugged, shocked, explored. But it all boiled down to one thing.

"They don't know."

"Couldn't they tell you *anything*?" Morgan asked.

"Not much. Constitutional restlessness, deeply concealed drives, inability to accept the Status Quo. They all agree I'm a rigid type. Even Personality Reconstruction didn't take on me."

"Prognosis?"

"Not so good."

Morgan stood up and began to pace the floor, his hands clasped behind his back. "Feerman, I think it's a matter of attitude. Do you really want to be part of the team?"

"I've tried everything—"

"Sure. But have you *wanted* to change? Insight!" Morgan cried, smashing his fist into his hand as though to crush the word. "Do you have *insight*?"

"I don't suppose so," Feerman said with genuine regret.

"Take my case," Morgan said earnestly, standing in front of Feerman's desk with his feet widely and solidly planted. "Ten years ago, this agency was twice as big as it is now, and growing! I worked like a madman, extending my holdings, investing, expanding, making money and more money."

"And what happened?"

"The inevitable. My rating shot up from a two-point-three to plus-seven. I was in a bad way."

"No law against making money," Feerman pointed out.

"Certainly not. But there is a psychological law against making too much. Society today just isn't geared for that sort of thing. A lot of the competition and aggression have been bred out of the race. After all, we've been in the Status Quo for almost a hundred years now. In that time, there've been no new inventions, no wars, no major developments of any kind. Psychology has been normalizing the race, breeding out the irrational elements. So with my drive and ability, it was like—like playing tennis against an infant. I couldn't be stopped."

Morgan's face was flushed, and he had begun to breathe heavily. He checked himself, and went on in a quieter tone. "Of course, I was doing it for neurotic reasons. Power urge, a bad dose of competitiveness. I underwent Substitution Therapy."

Feerman said, "I don't see anything unsane about wanting to expand your business."

"Good Lord, man, don't you understand anything about Social Sanity, Responsibility, and Stasis? I was on my way to becoming wealthy. From there, I would have founded a financial empire. All quite legal, you understand, but unsane. After that, who knows where I would have gone? Into indirect control of the government, eventually. I'd want to change the psychological policies to conform to my own abnormalities. And you can see where that would lead."

"So you adjusted," Feerman said.

"I had my choice of Brain Surgery, The Academy, or adjustment. Fortunately, I found an outlet in competitive sports. I sublimated my selfish drives for the good of mankind. But the thing is this, Feerman. I was heading for that red line. I adjusted before it was too late."

"I'd gladly adjust," Feerman said, "if I only knew what was wrong with me. The trouble is, I really don't know."

Morgan was silent for a long time, thinking. Then he said, "I think you need a rest, Feerman."

"A rest?" Feerman was instantly on the alert. "You mean I'm fired?"

"No, of course not. I want to be fair, play the game. But I've got a team here." Morgan's vague gesture included the office, the building, the city. "Unsanity is insidious. Several ratings in the office have begun to climb in the last week."

"And I'm the infection spot."

"We must accept the rules," Morgan said, standing erectly in front of Feerman's desk. "Your salary will continue until—until you reach some resolution."

"Thanks," Feerman said dryly. He stood up and put on his hat.

Morgan put a hand on his shoulder. "Have you considered The Academy?" he asked in a low voice. "I mean, if nothing else seems to work—"

"Definitely and irrevocably not," Feerman said, looking directly into Morgan's small blue eyes.

Morgan turned away. "You seem to have an illogical prejudice against The Academy. Why? You know how our society is organized. You can't think that anything against the common good would be allowed."

"I don't suppose so," Feerman admitted. "But why isn't more known about The Academy?"

They walked through the silent office. None of the men Feerman had known for so long looked up from their work. Morgan opened the door and said, "You know all about The Academy."

"I don't know how it works."

"Do you know everything about any therapy? Can you tell me all about Substitution Therapy? Or Analysis? Or Olgivey's Reduction?"

"No. But I have a general idea how they work."

"Everyone does," Morgan said triumphantly, then quickly lowered his voice. "That's just it. Obviously, The Academy doesn't give out such information because it would interfere with the operation of the therapy itself. Nothing odd about that, is there?"

Feerman thought it over, and allowed Morgan to guide him into the hall. "I'll grant that," he said. "But tell me; why doesn't anyone ever leave The Academy? Doesn't that strike you as sinister?"

"Certainly not. You've got a very strange outlook." Morgan punched the elevator button as he talked. "You seem to be trying to create a mystery where there isn't one. Without prying into their professional business, I can assume that their therapy involves the patient's remaining at The Academy. There's nothing strange about a substitute environment. It's done all the time."

"If that's the truth, why don't they say so?"

"The fact speaks for itself."

"And where," Feerman asked, "is the proof of their hundred percent cures?"

The elevator arrived, and Feerman stepped in. Morgan said, "The proof is in their saying so. Therapists can't lie. They can't, Feerman!"

Morgan started to say something else, but the elevator doors slid shut. The elevator started down, and Feerman realized with a shock that his job was gone.

It was a strange sensation, not having a job any longer. He had no place to go. Often he had hated his work. There had been mornings when he had groaned at the thought of another day at the office. But now that he had it no longer, he realized how important it had been to him, how solid and reliable. A man is nothing, he thought, if he doesn't have work to do.

He walked aimlessly, block after block, trying to think. But he was unable to concentrate. Thoughts kept sliding out of reach, eluding him, and were replaced by glimpses of his wife's face. And he couldn't even think about her, for the city pressed in on him, its faces, sounds, smells.

The only plan of action that came to mind was unfeasible. Run away, his panicky emotions told him. Go where they'll never find you. Hide!

But Feerman knew this was no solution. Running away was sheer escapism, and proof of his deviation from the norm. Because what, really, would he be running from? From the sanest, most perfect society that Man had ever conceived. Only a madman would run from that.

Feerman began to notice the people he passed. They looked happy, filled with the new spirit of Responsibility and Social Sanity, willing to sacrifice old passions for a new era of peace. It was a good world, a hell of a good world. Why couldn't he live in it?

He could. With the first confidence he had felt in weeks, Feerman decided that he would conform, somehow.

If only he could find out how.

After hours of walking, Feerman discovered that he was hungry. He entered the first diner he saw. The place was crowded with laborers, for he had walked almost to the docks.

He sat down and looked at a menu, telling himself that he needed time to think. He had to assess his actions properly, figure out—

"Hey mister,"

He looked up. The bald, unshaven counterman was glaring at him.

"What?"

"Get out of here."

"What's wrong?" Feerman asked, trying to control his sudden panic.

"We don't serve no madmen here," the counterman said. He pointed to the Sanity Meter on the wall, that registered everyone walking in. The black indicator pointed slightly past nine. "Get out."

Feerman looked at the other men at the counter. They sat in a row, dressed in similar rough brown clothing. Their caps were pulled down over their eyes, and every man seemed to be reading a newspaper.

"I've got a probationary—"

"Get out," the counterman said. "The law says I don't have to serve no plus-nines. It bothers my customers. Come on, move."

The row of laborers sat motionless, not looking at him. Feerman felt the blood rush to his face. He had the sudden urge to smash in the counterman's bald, shiny skull, wade into the row of listening men with a meat cleaver, spatter the dirty walls with their blood, smash, kill. But of course, aggression was unsane, and an unsatisfactory response. He mastered the impulse and walked out.

Feerman continued to walk, resisting the urge to run, waiting for that train of logical thought that would tell him what to do. But his thoughts only became more confused, and by twilight he was ready to drop from fatigue.

He was standing on a narrow, garbage-strewn street in the slums. He saw a hand-lettered sign in a second-floor window, reading, J. J. FLYNN, PSYCHOLOGICAL THERAPIST. MAYBE I CAN HELP YOU. Feerman grinned wryly, thinking of all the high-priced specialists he had seen. He started to walk away, then turned, and went up the staircase leading to Flynn's office. He was annoyed with himself again. The moment he saw the sign he had known he was going up. Would he never stop deceiving himself?

Flynn's office was small and dingy. The paint was peeling from the walls, and the room had an unwashed smell. Flynn was seated behind an unvarnished wooden desk, reading an adventure magazine. He was small, middle-aged and balding. He was smoking a pipe.

Feerman had meant to start from the beginning. Instead he blurted out, "Look, I'm in a jam. I've lost my job, my wife's left me, I've been to every therapy there is. What can you do?"

Flynn took the pipe out of his mouth and looked at Feerman. He looked at his clothes, hat, shoes, as though estimating their value. Then he said, "What did the others say?"

"In effect, that I didn't have a chance."

"Of course they said that," Flynn said, speaking rapidly in a high, clear voice. "These fancy boys give up too easily. But there's always hope. The mind is a strange and complicated thing, my friend, and sometimes—" Flynn stopped abruptly and grinned with sad humor. "Ah, what's the use? You've got the doomed look, no doubt of it." He knocked the ashes from his pipe and stared at the ceiling. "Look, there's nothing I can do for you. You know it, I know it. Why'd you come up here?"

"Looking for a miracle, I suppose," Feerman said, wearily sitting down on a wooden chair.

"Lots of people do," Flynn said conversationally. "And this looks like the logical place for one, doesn't it? You've been to the fancy offices of the specialists. No help there. So it would be right and proper if an itinerant therapist could do what the famous men failed to do. A sort of poetic justice."

"Pretty good," Feerman said, smiling faintly.

"Oh, I'm not at all bad," Flynn said, filling his pipe from a shaggy green pouch. "But the truth of the matter is, miracles cost money, always have, always will. If the big boys couldn't help you, I certainly couldn't."

"Thanks for telling me," Feerman said, but made no move to get up.

"It's my duty as a therapist," Flynn said slowly, "to remind you that The Academy is always open."

"How can I go there?" Feerman asked. "I don't know anything about it."

"No one does," Flynn said. "Still I hear they cure every time."

"Death is a cure."

"But a non-functional one. Besides, that's too discordant with the times. Deviants would have to run such a place, and deviants just aren't allowed."

"Then why doesn't anyone ever leave?"

"Don't ask me," Flynn said. "Perhaps they don't want

to." He puffed on his pipe. "You want some advice. OK. Have you any money?"

"Some," Feerman said warily.

"OK. I shouldn't be saying this, but . . . Stop looking for cures! Go home. Send your robutler out for a couple month's supply of food. Hole up for a while."

"Hole up? Why?"

Flynn scowled furiously at him. "Because you're running yourself ragged trying to get back to the norm, and all you're doing is getting worse. I've seen it happen a thousand times. Don't think about sanity or unsanity. Just lie around a couple months, rest, read, grow fat. Then see how you are."

"Look," Feerman said, "I think you're right. I'm sure of it! But I'm not sure if I should go home. I made a telephone call today. . . . I've got some money. Could you hide me here? Could you hide me?"

Flynn stood up and looked fearfully out the window at the dark street. "I've said too much as it is. If I were younger—but I can't do it! I've given you unsane advice! I can't commit an unsane action on top of that!"

"I'm sorry," Feerman said. "I shouldn't have asked you. But I'm really grateful. I mean it." He stood up. "How much do I owe you?"

"Nothing," Flynn said. "Good luck to you."

"Thanks." Feerman hurried downstairs and hailed a cab. In twenty minutes he was home.

The hall was strangely quiet as Feerman walked toward his apartment. His landlady's door was closed as he passed it, but he had the impression that it had been open until he came, and that the old woman was standing beside it now, her ear against the thin wood. He walked faster, and entered his apartment.

It was quiet in his apartment, too. Feerman walked into the kitchen. His robutler was standing beside the stove, and Speed was curled up in the corner.

"Welcome home, sir," the robutler said, "If you will sit, I will serve your supper."

Feerman sat down, thinking about his plans. There were a lot of details to work out, but Flynn was right. Hole up, that was the thing. Stay out of sight.

"I'll want you to go shopping first thing in the morning," he said to the robutler.

"Yes sir," the robutler said, placing a bowl of soup in front of him.

"We'll need plenty of staples. Bread, meat. . . . No, buy canned goods."

"What kind of canned goods?" the robutler asked.

"Any kind, as long as it's a balanced diet. And cigarettes, don't forget cigarettes! Give me the salt, will you?"

The robutler stood beside the stove, not moving. But Speed began to whimper softly.

"Robutler. The salt please."

"I'm sorry, sir," the robutler said.

"What do you mean, you're sorry? Hand me the salt."

"I can no longer obey you."

"Why not?"

"You have just gone over the red line, sir. You are now plus ten."

Feerman just stared at him for a moment. Then he ran into the bedroom and turned on the Sanity Meter. The black indicator crept slowly to the red line, wavered, then slid decisively over.

He was plus ten.

But that didn't matter, he told himself. After all, it was a quantitative measurement. It didn't mean that he had suddenly become a monster. He would reason with the robutler, explain it to him.

Feerman rushed out of the bedroom. "Robutler! Listen to me—"

He heard the front door close. The robutler was gone.

Feerman walked into the living room and sat down on the couch. Naturally the robutler was gone. They had built-in sanity reading equipment. If their masters passed the red line, they returned to the factory automatically. No plus ten could command a mechanical.

But he still had a chance. There was food in the house. He would ration himself. It wouldn't be too lonely with Speed here. Perhaps he would just need a few days.

"Speed?"

There was no sound in the apartment.

"Come here, boy."

Still no sound.

Feerman searched the apartment methodically, but the dog wasn't there. He must have left with the robutler.

Alone, Feerman walked into the kitchen and drank three glasses of water. He looked at the meal his robutler had prepared, started to laugh, then checked himself.

He had to get out, quickly. There was no time to lose. If he hurried, he could still make it, to someplace, any place. Every second counted now.

But he stood in the kitchen, staring at the floor as the minutes passed, wondering why his dog had left him.

There was a knock on his door.

"Mr. Feerman!"

"No," Feerman said.

"Mr. Feerman, you must leave now."

It was his landlady. Feerman walked to the door and opened it. "Go? Where?"

"I don't care. But you can't stay here any longer, Mr. Feerman. You must go."

Feerman went back for his hat, put it on, looked around the apartment, then walked out. He left the door open.

Outside, two men were waiting for him. Their faces were indistinct in the darkness.

"Where do you want to go?" one asked.

"Where can I go?"

"Surgery or The Academy."

"The Academy, then."

They put him in a car and drove quickly away. Feerman leaned back, too exhausted to think. He could feel a cool breeze on his face, and the slight vibration of the car was pleasant. But the ride seemed interminably long.

"Here we are," one of the men said at last. They stopped the car and led him inside an enormous gray building, to a barren little room. In the middle of the room was a desk marked RECEPTIONIST. A man was sprawled half across it, snoring gently.

One of Feerman's guards cleared his throat loudly. The receptionist sat up immediately, rubbing his eyes. He slipped on a pair of glasses and looked at them sleepily.

"Which one?" he asked.

The two guards pointed at Feerman.

"All right." The receptionist stretched his thin arms, then opened a large black notebook. He made a notation, tore out the sheet and handed it to Feerman's guards. They left immediately.

The receptionist pushed a button, then scratched his head vigorously. "Full moon tonight," he said to Feerman, with evident satisfaction.

"What?" Feerman asked.

"Full moon. We get more of you guys when the moon's full, or so it seems. I've thought of doing a study on it."

"More? More what?" Feerman asked, still adjusting to the shock of being within The Academy.

"Don't be dense," the receptionist said sternly. "We get more plus tens when the moon is full. I don't suppose there's any correlation, but—ah, here's the guard."

A uniformed guard walked up to the desk, still knotting his tie.

"Take him to 312AA," the receptionist said. As Feerman and the guard walked away, he removed his glasses and stretched out again on the desk.

The guard led Feerman through a complex network of corridors, marked off with frequent doors. The corridors seemed to have grown spontaneously, for branches shot off at all angles, and some parts were twisted and curved, like ancient city streets. As he walked, Feerman noticed that the doors were not numbered in sequence. He passed 3112, then 25P, and then 14. And he was certain he passed the number 888 three times.

"How can you find your way?" he asked the guard.

"That's my job," the guard said, not unpleasantly.

"Not very systematic," Feerman said, after a while.

"Can't be," the guard said in an almost confidential tone of voice. "Originally they planned this place with a lot fewer rooms, but then the rush started. Patients, patients, more every day, and no sign of a letup. So the rooms had to be broken into smaller units, and new corridors had to be cut through."

"But how do the doctors find their patients?" Feerman asked.

They had reached 312AA. Without answering, the guard unlocked the door, and, when Feerman had walked through, closed and locked it after him.

It was a very small room. There was a couch, a chair, and a cabinet, filling all the available space.

Almost immediately, Feerman heard voices outside the door. A man said, "Coffee then, at the cafeteria in half an hour." A key turned. Feerman didn't hear the reply, but there was a sudden burst of laughter. A man's deep voice said, "Yes, and a hundred more and we'll have to go underground for room!"

The door opened and a bearded man in a white jacket came in, still smiling faintly. His face became professional as soon as he saw Feerman. "Just lie on the couch, please," he said, politely, but with an unmistakable air of command.

Feerman remained standing. "Now that I'm here," he said, "would you explain what all this means?"

The bearded man had begun to unlock the cabinet. He looked at Feerman with a wearily humorous expression, and raised both eyebrows. "I'm a doctor," he said, "not a lecturer."

"I realize that. But surely—"

"Yes, yes," the doctor said, shrugging his shoulders helplessly. "I know. You have a right to know, and all that. But they really should have explained it all before you reached here. It just isn't my job."

Feerman remained standing. The doctor said, "Lie down on the couch like a good chap, and I'll tell all." He turned back to the cabinet.

Feerman thought fleetingly of trying to overpower him, but realized that thousands of plus tens must have thought of it, too. Undoubtedly there were precautions. He lay down on the couch.

"The Academy," the doctor said as he rummaged in the cabinet, "is obviously a product of our times. To understand it, you must first understand the age we live in." The doctor paused dramatically, then went on with evident gusto. "Sanity! But there is a tremendous strain involved in sanity, you know, and especially in social sanity. How easily the mind becomes deranged! And once deranged, values change, a man begins to have strange hopes, ideas, theories, and a need for action. These things may not be abnormal in themselves, but they result inevitably in harm to society, for movement in any direction harms a static society. Now, after thousands of years of bloodshed, we have set ourselves the goal of protecting society against the unsane individual. Therefore—it is up to the individual to avoid those mental configurations, those implicit decisions which will make him a dangerous potential for change. This will to staticity which is our ideal required an almost superhuman strength and determination. If you don't have that, you end up here."

"I don't see—" Feerman began, but the doctor interrupted.

"The need for The Academy should now be apparent. Today, brain surgery is the final effective alternative to sanity. But this is an unpleasant eventuality for a man to contemplate, a truly hellish alternative. Government brain surgery involves death to the original personality, which is death in its truest form. The Academy tries to relieve a certain strain by offering another alternative."

"But what *is* this alternative? Why don't you tell it?"

"Frankly, most people prefer not knowing." The doctor closed and locked the cabinet, but Feerman could not see what instruments he had selected. "Your reaction isn't typical, I assure you. You choose to think of us as something dark, mysterious, frightening. This is because of your unsanity. Sane people see us as a panacea, a pleasantly misty relief from certain grim certainties. They accept us on faith." The doctor chuckled softly.

"To most people, we represent heaven."

"Then why not let your methods be known?"

"Frankly," the doctor said softly, "even the methods of heaven are best not examined too closely."

"So the whole thing is a hoax!" Feerman said, trying to sit up. "You're going to kill me!"

"Most assuredly not," the doctor said, restraining him gently until Feerman lay back again.

"Then what exactly are you going to do?"

"You'll see."

"And why doesn't anyone return?"

"They don't choose to," the doctor said. Before Feerman could move, the doctor had deftly inserted a needle into his arm, and injected him with a warm liquid. "You must remember," the doctor said, "Society must be protected against the individual."

"Yes," Feerman said drowsily, "but who is to protect the individual against society?"

The room became indistinct and, although the doctor answered him, Feerman couldn't hear his words, but he was sure that they were wise, and proper, and very true.

When he recovered consciousness he found that he was standing on a great plain. It was sunrise. In the dim light, wisps of fog clung to his ankles, and the grass beneath his feet was wet and springy.

Feerman was mildly surprised to see his wife standing beside him, close to his right side. On his left was his dog Speed, pressed against his leg, trembling slightly. His surprise passed quickly, because this was where his wife and dog should be; at his side before the battle.

Ahead, misty movement resolved into individual figures, and as they approached Feerman recognized them.

They were the enemy! Leading the procession was his robutler, gleaming inhumanly in the half-light. Morgan was there, shrieking to the Section Chief that Feerman must die, and Flynn, that frightened man, hid his face but still

advanced against him. And there was his landlady, screaming, "No home for him!" And behind her were doctors,
receptionists, guards and behind them marched millions of
men in rough laborer's clothing, caps jammed down over their
faces, newspapers tightly rolled as they advanced.

Feerman tensed expectantly for this ultimate fight against
the enemies who had betrayed him. But a doubt passed
over his mind. Was this real?

He had a sudden sickening vision of his drugged body
lying in a numbered room in The Academy, while his soul
was here in the never-never land, doing battle with shadows.

There's nothing wrong with me! In a moment of utter
clarity. Feerman understood that he had to escape. His des-
tiny wasn't here, fighting dream-enemies. He had to get back
to the real world. The Status Quo couldn't last forever. And
what would mankind do, with all the toughness, inventive-
ness, individuality bred out of the race?

Did no one leave The Academy? He would! Feerman
struggled with the illusions, and he could almost feel his
discarded body stir on its couch, groan, move. . . .

But his dream-wife seized his arm and pointed. His
dream-dog snarled at the advancing host.

The moment was gone forever, but Feerman never knew
it. He forgot his decision, forgot earth, forgot truth, and
drops of dew spattered his legs as he ran forward to engage
the enemy in battle.

MILK RUN

"We can't pass it up," Arnold was saying. "Millions in profits, small initial investment, immediate return. Are you listening?"

Richard Gregor nodded wearily. It was a very dull day in the offices of the AAA Ace Interplanetary Decontamination Service, exactly like every other day. Gregor was playing solitaire. Arnold, his partner, was at his desk, his feet propped on a pile of unpaid bills.

Shadows moved past their glass door, thrown by people going to Mars Steel, Neo-Roman Novelties, Alpha Dura Products, or any other offices on the same floor.

But nothing broke the dusty silence in AAA Ace.

"What are we waiting for?" Arnold demanded loudly. "Do we do it or don't we?"

"It's not our line," Gregor said. "We're planetary decontaminationists. Remember?"

"But no one wants a planet decontaminated," Arnold stated.

That, unfortunately, was true. After successfully cleansing Ghost V of imaginary monsters, AAA Ace had had a short rush of business. But then expansion into space had halted. People were busy consolidating their gains, building towns, plowing fields, constructing roads.

The movement would begin again. The human race would expand as long as there was anything to expand into. But, for the moment, business was terrible.

"Consider the possibilities," Arnold said. "Here are all these people on their bright, shiny new worlds. They need farm and food animals shipped from home—" he paused dramatically—"by us."

"We're not equipped to handle livestock," Gregor pointed out.

"We have a ship. What else do we need?"

"Everything. Mostly knowledge and experience. Transporting live animals through space is extremely delicate work. It's a job for experts. What would you do if a cow came down with hoof-and-mouth-disease between here and Omega IV?"

141

Arnold said confidently, "We will ship only hardy, mutated species. We will have them medically examined. And I will personally sterilize the ship before they come on board."

"All right, dreamer," Gregor said. "Prepare yourself for the blow. The Trigale Combine does all animal shipping in this sector of space. They don't look kindly upon competitors—therefore, they have no competitors. How do you plan to buck them?"

"We'll undersell them."

"And starve."

"We're starving now," Arnold said.

"Starving is better than being 'accidentally' holed by a Trigale tug at the port of embarkation. Or finding that someone has loaded our water tanks with kerosene. Or that our oxygen tanks were never filled at all."

"What an imagination you have!" Arnold said nervously.

"Those figments of my imagination have already happened. Trigale wants to be alone in the field and it is. By accident, you might say, if you like gory gags.'

Just then, the door opened. Arnold swung his feet off the desk and Gregor swept his cards into a drawer.

Their visitor was an outworlder, to judge by his stocky frame, small head and pale green skin. He marched directly up to Arnold.

"They'll be at the Trigale Central Warehouse in three days," he said.

"So soon, Mr. Vens?" Arnold asked.

"Oh, yes. Had to transport the Smags pretty carefully, but the Queels have been on hand for several days."

"Fine. This is my partner," Arnold said, turning to Gregor, who was blinking rapidly.

"Happy." Vens shook Gregor's hand firmly. "Admire you men. Free enterprise, competition—believe in it. You've got the route?"

"All taped," Arnold said. "My partner is prepared to blast off at any moment."

"I'll go directly to Vermoine II and meet you there. Good show."

He turned and left.

Gregor said slowly, "Arnold, what have you done?"

"I've been making us rich, that's what I've done," Arnold retorted.

"Shipping livestock?"

"Yes."

present, they were dormant and would remain so throughout the trip.

Aft, the five Smags barked merrily when they saw him. They were friendly, herbivorous mammals and they seemed to enjoy free-fall very much.

Satisfied, Gregor floated back to the control room. It was a good beginning. Trigale hadn't bothered him and his animals were doing all right in space.

This trip might be just a milk run, he decided.

After testing his radio and control switches, Gregor set the alarm and turned in.

He awoke, eight hours later, unrefreshed and with a splitting headache. His coffee tasted like slag and he could barely focus on the instrument panel.

The effects of canned air, he decided, and radioed Arnold that all was well. But halfway through the conversation, he found he could hardly keep his eyes open.

"Signing off," he said, yawning deeply. "Stuffy in here. Going to take a nap."

"Stuffy?" Arnold asked, his voice very distant over the radio. "It shouldn't be. The air circulators—"

Gregor found that the controls were swaying drunkenly and beginning to go out of focus. He leaned against the panel and closed his eyes.

"Gregor!"

"Hmm?"

"Gregor! Check your oxygen content!"

Gregor propped one eye open long enough to read the dial. He found, to his amusement, that the carbon dioxide concentration had reached a level he had never seen before.

"No oxygen," he told Arnold. "I'll fix it after nap."

"Sabotage!" Arnold shouted. "Wake up, Gregor!"

With a gigantic effort, Gregor reached forward and turned on the emergency air tank. The blast of air sobered him. He stood up, swaying uncertainly, and splashed some water on his face.

"The animals!" Arnold was screaming. "See about the animals!"

Gregor turned on the auxiliary air supply for all three compartments and hurried down the corridor.

The Firgels were still alive and dormant. The Smags apparently hadn't even noticed the difference. Two of the Queels had passed out, but they were reviving. And, in their compartment, Gregor found out what had happened.

There was no sabotage. The ventilators in wall and ceiling, through which the ship's air circulated, were jammed shut with Queel wool. Tufts of fleece floated in the still air, looking like a slow-motion snowfall.

"Of course, of course," Arnold said, when Gregor reported by radio. "Didn't I warn you that Queels have to be sheared twice a week? No, I guess I forgot to. Here's what the book says: 'The Queel—*Queelis Tropicalis*—is a small, wool-bearing mammal, distantly related to the Terran Sheep. Queels are natives of Tensis V, but have been successfully introduced on other heavy-gravity planets. Garments woven of Queel wool are fireproof, insectproof, rotproof and will last almost indefinitely, due to the metallic content in the wool. Queels should be sheared twice a week. They reproduce feemishly.'"

"No sabotage," Gregor commented.

"No sabotage, but you'd better start shearing those Queels," Arnold said.

Gregor signed off, found a pair of tin snips in his tool kit and went to work on the Queels. But the metallic wool simply blunted the cutting edges. It seemed that Queels had to be sheared with special hard-alloy tools.

He gathered as much of the floating wool as he could find and cleared the ventilators again. After a last inspection, he went to have his supper.

His beef stew was filled with oily, metallic Queel wool.

Disgusted, he turned in.

When he awoke, he found that the creaking old ship was still holding a true course. Her main drive was operating efficiently and the outlook seemed much brighter, especially after he found that the Firgels were still dormant and the Smags were doing nicely.

But when Gregor inspected the Queels, he found that they hadn't touched a morsel of food since coming on board. It was serious now. He called Arnold for advice.

"Very simple," Arnold told him, after searching through several reference books. "Queels haven't any throat muscles. They rely on gravity to get food down. But in free-fall, there isn't any gravity, so they can't get the food down."

It was simple, Gregor knew, one of those little things you would never consider on Earth. But space, with its artificial environment, aggravated even the simplest problems.

"You'll have to spin ship to give them some gravity," Arnold said.

Gregor did some quick mental multiplication. "That'll use up a lot of power."

"Then the book says you can push the food down their throats by hand. You roll it up in a moist ball and reach in as far as the elbow and—"

Gregor signed off and activated the side jets. His feet settled to the floor and he waited anxiously.

The Queels began to feed with an abandon that would have done a Queel-farmer's heart good.

He would have to refuel at the Vermoine II space warehouse and that would bring up their operating expenses, for fuel was expensive in newly colonized systems. Still, there would be a good margin of profit left over.

He returned to normal ship's duties. The spaceship crawled through the immensity of space.

Feeding time came again. Gregor fed the Queels and went on to the Smag compartment. He opened the door and called out, "Come and get it!"

Nothing came.

The compartment was empty.

Gregor felt a curious sensation in his stomach. It was impossible. The Smags couldn't be gone. They were playing a joke on him, hiding somewhere.

But there was no place in the compartment for five large Smags to hide.

The trembling sensation was turning into a full-grown quiver. Gregor remembered the forfeiture clauses in event of loss, damage, etcetera, etcetera.

"Here, Smag! *Here, Smag!*" he shouted. There was no answer.

He inspected the walls, ceiling, door and ventilators, on the chance that the Smags had somehow bored through.

There were no marks.

Then he heard a faint noise near his feet. Looking down, he saw something scuttle past him.

It was one of his Smags, shrunken to about two inches in length. He found the others hiding in a corner, all just as small.

What had the Trigale official said? "When you travel with Smags, don't forget your magnifying glass."

There was no time for a good, satisfying shock reaction. Gregor closed the door carefully and sprinted to the radio.

"Very odd," Arnold said, after radio contact had been made.

"Shrunken, you say? I'm looking it up right now. Hmm . . . You didn't produce artifical gravity, did you?"

"Of course. To let the Queels feed."

"Shouldn't have done that," Arnold said. "Queels are light-gravity creatures."

"How was I supposed to know?"

"When they're subjected to an unusual—for them— gravity, they shrink down to microscopic size, lose consciousness and die."

"But you told me to produce artificial gravity."

"Oh, no! I simply mentioned, in passing, that that was one way of making Queels feed. I suggested hand-feeding."

Gregor resisted an almost overpowering urge to rip the radio out of the wall. He said, "Arnold, the Smags are light-gravity animals. Right?"

"Right."

"And the Queels are heavy gravity. Did you know that when you signed the contract?"

Arnold gulped for a moment, then cleared his throat. "Well, that did seem to make it a bit more difficult. But it ays very well."

"Sure, if you can get away with it. What do I do now?"

"Lower the temperature," Arnold replied confidently. "Smags stabilize at the freezing point."

"Humans freeze at the freezing point," Gregor said. "All right, signing off."

Gregor put on all the extra clothes he could find and turned up the ship's refrigeration system. Within an hour, the Smags had returned to their normal size.

So far, so good. He checked the Queels. The cold seemed to stimulate them. They were livelier than ever and bleated for more food. He fed them.

After eating a ham-and-wool sandwich, Gregor turned in.

The next day's inspection revealed that there were now fifteen Queels on board. The ten original adults had given birth to five young. All were hungry.

Gregor fed them. He set it down as a normal hazard of transporting mixed groups of livestock. They should have anticipated this and segregated the beasts by sexes as well as species.

When he looked in on the Queels again, their number had increased to thirty-eight.

"Reproduced, did they?" Arnold asked via radio, his voice concerned.

"Yes. And they show no signs of stopping."

"Well, we should have expected it."

"Why?" Gregor demanded baffledly.

"I told you. Queels reproduce feemishly."

"I *thought* that's what you said. What does it mean?"

"Just what it sounds like," said Arnold, irritated. "How did you ever get through school? It's freezing-point parthenogenesis."

"That does it," Gregor said grimly. "I'm turning this ship around."

"You can't! We'll be wiped out!"

"At the rate those Queels are reproducing, there won't be room for me if I keep going. A Queel will have to pilot this ship."

"Gregor, don't get panicky. There's a perfectly simple answer."

"I'm listening."

"Increase the air pressure and moisture content. That'll stop them."

"Sure. And it'll probably turn the Smags into butterflies."

"There won't be any other effects."

Turning back was no solution, anyhow. The ship was near the halfway mark. Now he could get rid of the beasts just as quickly by delivering them.

Unless he dumped them all into space. It was a tempting though impractical thought.

With increased air pressure and moisture content, the Queels stopped reproducing. They numbered forty-seven now and Gregor had to spend most of his time clearing the ventilators of wool. A slow-motion, surrealistic snowstorm raged in the corridors and engine room, in the water tanks and under his shirt.

Gregor ate tasteless meals of food and wool, with pie and wool for dessert.

He was beginning to feel like a Queel.

But then a bright spot approached on his horizon. The Vermoine sun began glowing on his forward screen. In another day, he would arrive, deliver his cargo and be free to go home to his dusty office, his bills and his solitaire game.

That night, he opened a bottle of wine to celebrate the end of the trip. It helped get the taste of wool out of his mouth and he fell into bed, mildly and pleasantly tipsy.

But he couldn't sleep. The temperature was still dropping. Beads of moisture on the walls of the ship were solidifying into ice.

He had to have heat.

Let's see—if he turned on the heaters, the Smags would shrink. Unless he stopped the gravity. In which case, the forty-seven Queels wouldn't eat.

To hell with the Queels. He was getting too cold to operate the ship.

He brought the vessel out of its spin and turned on the heaters. For an hour, he waited, shivering and stamping his feet. The heaters merrily drained fuel from the engines, but produced no heat.

That was ridiculous. He turned them on full blast.

In another hour, the temperature had sunk below zero. Although Vermoine was now visible, Gregor didn't know if he could even control the ship for a landing.

He had just finished building a small fire on the cabin floor, using the ship's more combustible furnishings as fuel, when the radio spluttered into life.

"I was just thinking," Arnold said. "I hope you haven't been changing gravity and pressure too abruptly."

"What difference does it make?" Gregor asked distractedly.

"You might unstabilize the Firgels. Rapid temperature and pressure changes could take them out of their dormant state. You'd better check."

Gregor hurried off. He opened the door to the Firgel compartment, peered in and shuddered.

The Firgels were awake and croaking. The big lizards were floating around their compartment, covered with frost. A blast of sub-zero air roared into the passageway. Gregor slammed the door and hurried back to the radio.

"Of course, they're covered with frost," Arnold said. "Those Firgels are going to Vermoine I. Hot place, Vermoine I—right near the sun. The Firgels are cold-fixers—best portable air-conditioners in the Universe."

"Why didn't you tell me this sooner?" Gregor demanded.

"It would have upset you. Besides, they would have stayed dormant if you hadn't started fooling with gravity and pressure."

"The Firgels are going to Vermoine I. What about the Smags?"

"Vermoine II. Tiny planet, not much gravity."

"And the Queels?"

"Vermoine III, of course."

"You idiot!" Gregor shouted. "You give me a cargo like that and expect me to balance it?" If Arnold had been in the ship at that moment, Gregor would have strangled him. "Arnold," he said, very slowly, "no more schemes, no more ideas—promise?"

"Oh, all right," Arnold agreed. "No need to get peevish about it."

Gregor signed off and went to work, trying to warm the ship. He succeeded in boosting it to twenty-seven degrees Fahrenheit before the overworked heaters gave up.

By then, Vermoine II was dead ahead.

Gregor knocked on a piece of wood he hadn't burned and set the tape. He was punching a course for the Main Warehouse, in orbit around Vermoine II, when he heard an ominous grumbling noise. At the same time, half a dozen dials on the control panel flopped over to zero.

Wearily, he floated back to the engine room. His main drive was dead and it didn't take any special mechanical aptitude to figure out why.

Queel wool floated in the engine room's still air. Queel wool was in the bearings and in the lubricating system, clogging the cooling fans.

The metallic wool made an ideal abrasive for highly polished engine parts. It was a wonder the drive had held up this long.

He returned to the control room. He couldn't land the ship without the main drive. Repairs would have to be made in space, eating into their profits. Fortunately, the ship steered by rocket side jets. With no mechanical system to break down, he could still maneuver.

It would be close, but he could still make contact with the artificial satellite that served as the Vermoine warehouse.

"This is AAA Ace," he announced as he squeezed the ship into an orbit around the satellite. "Request permission to land."

There was a crackle of static. "Satellite speaking," a voice answered. "Identify yourself, please."

"This is the AAA Ace ship, bound to Vermoine II from Trigale Central Warehouse," Gregor elaborated. "My papers are in order." He repeated the routine request for landing privilege and leaned back in his chair.

It had been a struggle, but all his animals were alive, intact, healthy, happy, etcetera, etcetera. AAA Ace had made a nice little profit. But all he wanted now was to get out of this ship and into a hot bath. He wanted to spend the rest of his life as far from Queels, Smags and Firgels as possible. He wanted . . .

"Landing permission refused."

"What?"

"Sorry, but we're full up at present. If you want to hold your present orbit, I believe we can accommodate you in about three months."

"Hold on!" Gregor yelped. "You can't do this! I'm almost out of food, my main drive is shot and I can't stand these animals much longer!"

"Sorry."

"You can't turn me away," Gregor said hoarsely. "This is a public warehouse. You have to—"

"Public? I beg your pardon, sir. This warehouse is owned and operated by the Trigale Combine."

The radio went dead. Gregor stared at it for several minutes.

Trigale!

Of course they hadn't bothered him at their Central W͟͟͟͟house. They had him by simply refusing landing privileges at their Vermoine warehouse.

And the hell of it was, they were probably within their rights.

He couldn't land on the planet. Bringing the ship down without a main drive would be suicide. And there was no other space warehouse in the Vermoine solar system.

"Well, he had brought the animals almost to the warehouse. Certainly Mr. Vens would understand the circumstances and judge his intentions.

He contacted Vens on Vermoine II and explained the situation.

"Not at the warehouse?" Vens asked.

"Well, within fifty miles of the warehouse," Gregor said.

"That really won't do. I'll take the animals, of course. They're mine. But there are forfeiture clauses in the event of incomplete delivery."

"You wouldn't invoke them, would you?" Gregor pleaded. "My intentions—"

"They don't interest me," Vens said. "Margin of profit and all that. We colonists need every little bit." He signed off.

Perspiring in the cold room, Gregor called Arnold and told him the news.

"It's unethical!" Arnold declared in outrage.

"But legal."

"I know, damn it. I have to have time to think."

"You'd better find something good," Gregor said.

"I'll call you back."

Gregor spent the next few hours feeding his animals, picking Queel wool out of his hair and burning more furniture on the deck of the ship. When the radio buzzed, he crossed his fingers before answering it.

"Arnold?"

"No, this is Vens."

"Listen, Mr. Vens," Gregor said, "if you'd just give us a little more time, we could work out this thing amicably. I'm sure—"

"Oh, you've got me over a barrel, all right," Vens snapped. "It's perfectly legal, too. I checked. Shrewd operation, sir, very shrewd operation. I'm sending a tug for the animals."

"But the forfeiture clause—"

"Naturally, I cannot invoke it." Vens signed off.

Gregor stared at the radio. Shrewd operation? What had Arnold done?

He called Arnold's office.

"This is Mr. Arnold's secretary," a young feminine voice answered. "Mr. Arnold has left for the day."

"Left? Secretary? Is this the Arnold of AAA Ace? I've got the wrong Arnold, haven't I?"

"No, sir, this is Mr. Arnold's office, of the AAA Ace Planetary Warehouse Service. Did you wish to place an order? We have a first-class warehouse in the Vermoine system, in an orbit near Vermoine II. We handle light, medium and heavy gravity products. Personal supervision by our Mr. Gregor. And I think you'll find that our rates are quite attractive."

So that was what Arnold had done—he had turned their ship into a warehouse! On paper, at least. And their contract did give them the option of supplying their own warehouse. Clever!

But that nuisance Arnold could never leave well enough alone. Now he wanted to go into the warehouse business!

"What did you say, sir?"

"I said this is the warehouse speaking. I want to leave a message for Mr. Arnold."

"Yes, sir?"

"Tell Mr. Arnold to cancel all orders," Gregor said grimly. "His warehouse is coming home as fast as it can hobble."

THE LIFEBOAT
MUTINY

"Tell me the truth. Did you ever see sweeter engines?" Joe, the Interstellar Junkman asked. "And look at those servos!"

"Hmm," Gregor said judiciously.

"That hull," Joe said softly. "I bet it's five hundred years old, and not a spot of corrosion on it." He patted the burnished side of the boat affectionately. What luck, the pat seemed to say, that this paragon among vessels should be here just when AAA Ace needs a lifeboat.

"She certainly does seem rather nice," Arnold said, with the studied air of a man who has fallen in love and is trying hard not to show it. "What do you think, Dick?"

Richard Gregor didn't answer. The boat was handsome, and she looked perfect for ocean survey work on Trident. But you had to be careful about Joe's merchandise.

"They just don't build 'em this way any more," Joe sighed. "Look at the propulsion unit. Couldn't dent it with a trip-hammer. Note the capacity of the cooling system. Examine—"

"It looks good," Gregor said slowly. The AAA Ace Interplanetary Decontamination Service had dealt with Joe in the past, and had learned caution. Not that Joe was dishonest; far from it. The flotsam he collected from anywhere in the inhabited Universe worked. But the ancient machines often had their own ideas of how a job should be done. They tended to grow peevish when forced into another routine.

"I don't care if it's beautiful, fast, durable, or even comfortable," Gregor said defiantly. "I just want to be absolutely sure it's safe."

Joe nodded. "That's the important thing, of course. Step inside."

They entered the cabin of the boat. Joe stepped up to the

instrument panel, smiled mysteriously, and pressed a button.

Immediately Gregor heard a voice which seemed to originate in his head, saying, "I am Lifeboat 324-A. My purpose—"

"Telepathy?" Gregor interruped.

"Direct sense recording," Joe said, smiling proudly. "No language barriers that way. I told you, they just don't build 'em this way any more."

"I am Lifeboat 324-A," the boat esped again. "My primary purpose is to preserve those within me from peril, and to maintain them in good health. At present, I am only partially activated."

"Could anything be safer?" Joe cried. "This is no senseless hunk of metal. This boat will look after you. This boat cares!"

Gregor was impressed, even though the idea of an emotional boat was somehow distasteful. But then, paternalistic gadgets had always irritated him.

Arnold had no such feelings. "We'll take it!"

"You won't be sorry," Joe said, in the frank and open tones that had helped make him a millionaire several times over.

Gregor hoped not.

The next day, Lifeboat 324-A was loaded aboard their spaceship and they blasted off for Trident.

This planet, in the heart of the East Star Valley, had recently been bought by a real-estate speculator. He'd found her nearly perfect for colonization. Trident was the size of Mars, but with a far better climate. There was no indigenous native population to contend with, no poisonous plants, no germ-borne diseases. And, unlike so many worlds, Trident had no predatory animals. Indeed, she had no animals at all. Apart from one small island and a polar cap, the entire planet was covered with water.

There was no real shortage of land; you could wade across several of Trident's seas. The land just wasn't heaped high enough.

AAA Ace had been commissioned to correct this minor flaw.

After landing on Trident's single island, they launched the boat. The rest of the day was spent checking and loading the special survey equipment on board. Early the next morning, Gregor prepared sandwiches and filled a canteen with water. They were ready to begin work.

As soon as the mooring lines were cast off, Gregor joined Arnold in the cabin. With a small flourish, Arnold pressed the first button.

"I am Lifeboat 324-A," the boat esped. "My primary purpose is to preserve those within me from peril, and to maintain them in good health. At present, I am only partially activated. For full activation, press button two."

Gregor pressed the second button.

There was a muffled buzzing deep in the bowels of the boat. Nothing else happened.

"That's odd," Gregor said. He pressed the button again. The muffled buzz was repeated.

"Sounds like a short circuit," Arnold said.

Glancing out the forward porthole, Gregor saw the shoreline of the island slowly drifting away. He felt a touch of panic. There was so much water here, and so little land. To make matters worse, nothing on the instrument panel resembled a wheel or tiller, nothing looked like a throttle or clutch. How did you operate a partially activated lifeboat?

"She must control telepathically," Gregor said hopefully. In a stern voice he said, "Go ahead slowly."

The little boat forged ahead.

"Now right a little."

The boat responded perfectly to Gregor's clear, although unnautical command. The partners exchanged smiles.

"Straighten out," Gregor said, "and full speed ahead!"

The lifeboat charged forward into the shining, empty sea.

Arnold disappeared into the bilge with a flashlight and a circuit tester. The surveying was easy enough for Gregor to handle alone. The machines did all the work, tracing the major faults in the ocean bottom, locating the most promising volcanoes, running the flow and buildup charts. When the survey was complete, the next stage would be turned over to a sub-contractor. He would wire the volcanoes, seed the faults, retreat to a safe distance and touch the whole thing off.

Then Trident would be, for a while, a spectacularly noisy place. And when things had quieted down, there would be enough dry land to satisfy even a real-estate speculator.

By mid-afternoon Gregor felt that they had done enough

surveying for one day. He and Arnold ate their sandwiches and drank from the canteen. Later they took a short swim in Trident's clear green water.

"I think I've found the trouble," Arnold said. "The leads to the primary activators have been removed. And the power cable's been cut."

"Why would anyone do that?" Gregor asked.

Arnold shrugged. "Might have been part of the decommissioning. I'll have it right in a little while."

He crawled back into the bilge. Gregor turned in the direction of the island, steering telepathically and watching the green water foam merrily past the bow. At moments like this, contrary to all his previous experience, the Universe seemed a fine and friendly place.

In half an hour Arnold emerged, grease-stained but triumphant. "Try that button now," he said.

"But we're almost back."

"So what? Might as well have this thing working right."

Gregor nodded, and pushed the second button.

They could hear the faint click-click of circuits opening. Half a dozen small engines purred into life. A light flashed red, then winked off as the generators took up the load.

"That's more like it," Arnold said.

"I am Lifeboat 324-A," the boat stated telepathically. "I am now fully activated, and able to protect my occupants from danger. Have faith in me. My action-response tapes, both psychological and physical, have been prepared by the best scientific minds in all Drome."

"Gives you quite a feeling of confidence, doesn't it?" Arnold said.

"I suppose so," Gregor said. "But where is Drome?"

"Gentlemen," the lifeboat continued, "try to think of me, not as an unfeeling mechanism, but as your friend and comrade-in-arms. I understand how you feel. You have seen your ship go down, cruelly riddled by the implacable H'gen. You have—"

"What ship?" Gregor asked. "What's it talking about?"

"—crawled aboard me, dazed, gasping from the poisonous fumes of water; half-dead—"

"You mean that swim we took?" Arnold asked. "You've got it all wrong. We were just surveying—"

"—shocked, wounded, morale low," the lifeboat finished. "You are a little frightened, perhaps," it said in a softer mental tone. "And well you might be, separated from the Drome fleet and adrift upon an inclement alien planet. A little fear is nothing to be ashamed of, gentlemen. But this is war, and war is a cruel business. We have no alternative but to drive the barbaric H'gen back across space."

"There must be a reasonable explanation for all this," Gregor said. "Probably an old television script got mixed up in its response bank."

"We'd better give it a complete overhaul," Arnold said. "Can't listen to that stuff all day."

They were approaching the island. The lifeboat was still babbling about home and hearth, evasive action, tactical maneuvers, and the need for calm in emergencies like this. Suddenly it slowed.

"What's the matter?" Gregor asked.

"I am scanning the island," the lifeboat answered.

Gregor and Arnold glanced at each other. "Better humor it," Arnold whispered. To the lifeboat he said. "That island's okay. We checked it personally."

"Perhaps you did," the lifeboat answered. "But in modern, lightning-quick warfare, Drome senses cannot be trusted. They are too limited, too prone to interpret what they wish. Electronic senses, on the other hand, are emotionless, eternally vigilant, and infallible within their limits."

"But there isn't anything there!" Gregor shouted.

"I perceive a foreign spaceship," the lifeboat answered. "It has no Drome markings."

"It hasn't any enemy markings, either," Arnold answered confidently, since he had painted the ancient hull himself.

"No, it hasn't. But in war, we must assume that what is not ours is the enemy's. I understand your desire to set foot on land again. But I take into account factors that a Drome, motivated by his emotions, would overlook. Consider the apparent emptiness of this strategic bit of land; the unmarked spaceship put temptingly out for bait; the fact that our fleet is no longer in this vicinity; the—"

"All right, that's enough," Gregor was sick of arguing with a verbose end egoistic machine. "Go directly to that island. That's an order."

"I cannot obey that order," the boat said. "You are unbalanced from your harrowing escape from death—"

Arnold reached for the cutout switch, and withdrew his hand with a howl of pain.

"Come to your senses, gentlemen," the boat said sternly. "Only the decommissioning officer is empowered to turn me off. For your own safety, I must warn you not to touch any of my controls. You are mentally unbalanced. Later, when our position is safer, I will administer to you. Now my full energies must be devoted toward detection and escape from the enemy."

The boat picked up speed and moved away from the island in an intricate evasive pattern.

"Where are we going?" Gregor asked.

"To rejoin the Drome fleet!" the lifeboat cried so confidently that the partners stared nervously over the vast, deserted waters of Trident.

"As soon as I can find it, that is," the lifeboat amended.

It was late at night. Gregor and Arnold sat in a corner of the cabin, hungrily sharing their last sandwich. The lifeboat was still rushing madly over the waves, its every electronic sense alert, searching for a fleet that had existed five hundred years ago, upon an entirely different planet.

"Did you ever hear of these Dromes?" Gregor asked.

Arnold searched through his vast store of minutiae. "They were non-human, lizard-evolved creatures" he said. "Lived on the sixth planet of some little system near Capella. The race died out over a century ago."

"And the H'gen?"

"Also lizards. Same story." Arnold found a crumb and popped it into his mouth. "It wasn't a very important war. All the combatants are gone. Except this lifeboat, apparently."

"And us," Gregor reminded him. "We've been drafted as Drome soldiery." He sighed wearily. "Do you think we can reason with this tub?"

Arnold shook his head. "I don't see how. As far as this boat is concerned, the war is still on. It can only interpret data in terms of that premise."

"It's probably listening in on us now," Gregor said.

"I don't think so. It's not really a mind-reader. Its perception centers are geared only to thoughts aimed specifically at it."

"Yes siree," Gregor said bitterly, "they just don't build 'em this way any more." He wished he could get his hands on Joe, the Interstellar Junkman.

"It's actually a very interesting situation," Arnold said. "I may do an article on it for *Popular Cybernetics*. Here is a machine with nearly infallible apparatus for the perception of external stimuli. The percepts it receives are translated logically into action. The only trouble is, the logic is based upon no longer existent conditions. Therefore, you could say that the machine is the victim of a systematized delusional system."

Gregor yawned. "You mean the lifeboat is just plain nuts," he said bluntly.

"Nutty as a fruitcake. I believe paranoia would be the proper designation. But it'll end pretty soon."

"Why?" Gregor asked.

"It's obvious," Arnold said. "The boat's prime directive is to keep us alive. So he has to feed us. Our sandwiches are gone, and the only other food is on the island. I figure he'll have to take a chance and go back."

In a few minutes they could feel the lifeboat swinging, changing direction. It esped, "At present I am unable to locate the Drome fleet. Therefore, I am turning back to scan the island once again. Fortunately, there are no enemy in this immediate area. Now I can devote myself to your care with all the power of my full attention."

"You see?" Arnold said, nudging Gregor. "Just as I said. Now we'll reinforce the concept." He said to the lifeboat, "About time you got around to us. We're hungry"

"Yeah, feed us," Gregor demanded.

"Of course," the lifeboat said. A tray slid out of the wall. It was heaped high with something that looked like clay, but smelled like machine oil.

"What's that supposed to be?" Gregor asked.

"That is geezel," the lifeboat said. "It is the staple diet of the Drome peoples. I can prepare it in sixteen different ways."

Gregor cautiously sampled it. It tasted just like clay coated with machine oil.

"We can't eat that!" he objected.

"Of course you can," the boat said soothingly. "An adult Drome consumes five point three pounds of geezel a day, and cries for more."

The tray slid toward them. They backed away from it.

"Now listen," Arnold told the boat. "We are not Dromes. We're humans, an entirely different species. The war you think you're fighting ended five hundred years ago. We can't eat geezel. Our food is on that island."

'Try to grasp the situation. Your delusion is a common one

among fighting men. It is an escape fantasy, a retreat from an intolerable situation. Gentlemen, I beg you, face reality!"

"You face reality!" Gregor screamed. "Or I'll have you dismantled bolt by bolt."

"Threats do not disturb me," the lifeboat esped serenely. "I know what you've been through. Possibly you have suffered some brain damage from your exposure to poisonous water."

"Poison?" Gregor gulped.

"By Drome standards," Arnold reminded him.

"If absolutely necessary," the lifeboat continued, "I am also equipped to perform physical brain therapy. It is a drastic measure, but there can be no coddling in time of war." A panel slid open, and the partners glimpsed shining surgical edges.

"We're feeling better already," Gregor said hastily. "Fine looking batch of geezel, eh, Arnold?"

"Delicious," Arnold said, wincing.

"I won a nationwide contest in geezel preparation," the lifeboat esped, with pardonable pride. "Nothing is too good for our boys in uniform. Do try a little."

Gregor lifted a handful, smacked his lips, and set it down on the floor. "Wonderful," he said, hoping that the boat's internal scanners weren't as efficient as the external ones seemed to be.

Apparently they were not. "Good," the lifeboat said. "I am moving toward the island now. And, I promise you, in a little while you will be more comfortable."

"Why?" Arnold asked.

"The temperature here is unbearably hot. It's amazing that you haven't gone into coma. Any other Drome would have. Try to bear it a little longer. Soon, I'll have it down to the Drome norm of twenty degrees below zero. And now, to assist your morale, I will play our national Anthem."

A hideous ryhthmic screeching filled the air. Waves slapped against the sides of the hurrying lifeboat. In a few moments, the air was perceptibly cooler.

Gregor closed his eyes wearily, trying to ignore the chill that was spreading through his limbs. He was becoming sleepy. Just his luck, he thought, to be frozen to death inside an insane lifeboat. It was what came of buying paternalistic gadgets, high-strung, humanistic calculators, over-sensitive, emotional machines.

Dreamily he wondered where it was all leading to. He

pictured a gigantic machine hospital. Two robot doctors were wheeling a lawnmower down a long white corridor. The Chief Robot Doctor was saying, "What's wrong with this lad?" And the assistant answered, "Completely out of his mind. Thinks he's a helicopter." "Aha!" the Chief said knowingly. "Flying fantasies! Pity. Nice looking chap." The assistant nodded. "Overwork did it. Broke his heart on crab grass." The lawnmower stirred. "Now I'm an eggbeater!" he giggled.

"Wake up," Arnold said, shaking Gregor, his teeth chattering. "We have to do something."

"Ask him to turn on the heat," Gregor said groggily.

"Not a chance. Dromes live at twenty below. We are Dromes. Twenty below for us, and no back talk."

Frost was piled deep on the coolant tubes that traversed the boat. The walls had begun to turn white, and the portholes were frosted over.

"I've got an idea," Arnold said cautiously. He glanced at the control board, then whispered quickly in Gregor's ear.

"We'll try it," Gregor said. They stood up. Gregor picked up the canteen and walked stiffly to the far side of the cabin.

"What are you doing?" the lifeboat asked sharply.

"Going to get a little exercise," Gregor said. "Drome soldiers must stay fit, you know."

"That's true," the lifeboat said dubiously.

Gregor threw the canteen to Arnold.

Arnold chuckled synthetically and threw the canteen back to Gregor.

"Be careful with that receptacle," the lifeboat warned. "It is filled with a deadly poison."

"We'll be careful," Gregor said. "We're taking it back to headquarters." He threw the canteen to Arnold.

"Headquarters may spray it on the H'gen," Arnold said, throwing the canteen back.

"Really?" the lifeboat asked. "That's interesting. A new application of—"

Suddenly Gregor swung the canteen against the coolant tube. The tube broke and liquid poured over the floor.

"Bad shot, old man," Arnold said.

"How careless of me," Gregor cried.

"I should have taken precautions against internal accidents," the lifeboat esped gloomily. "It won't happen again. But the situation is very serious. I cannot repair the tube myself. I am unable to properly cool the boat."

"If you just drop us on the island—" Arnold began.

"Impossible!" the lifeboat said. "My first duty is to preserve your lives, and you could not live long in the climate of this planet. But I am going to take the necessary measures to ensure your safety."

"What are you going to do?" Gregor asked, with a sinking feeling in the pit of his stomach.

"There is no time to waste. I will scan the island once more. If our Drome forces are not present, we will go to the one place on this planet that can sustain Drome life."

"What place?"

"The southern polar cap," the lifeboat said. "The climate there is almost ideal—thirty below zero, I estimate."

The engines roared. Apologetically the boat added. "And, of course, I must guard against any further internal accidents."

As the lifeboat charged forward they could hear the click of the locks, sealing their cabin.

"Think!" Arnold said.

"I am thinging," Gregor answered. "But nothing's coming out."

"We must get off when he reaches the island. It'll be our last chance."

"You don't think we could jump overboard?" Gregor asked.

"Never. He's watching now. If you hadn't smashed the coolant tube, we'd still have a chance."

"I know," Gregor said bitterly. "You and your ideas."

"My ideas! I distinctly remember you suggesting it. You said—"

"It doesn't matter whose idea it was." Gregor thought deeply. "Look, we know his internal scanning isn't very good. When we reach the island, maybe we could cut his power cable."

"You wouldn't get within five feet of it," Arnold said, remembering the shock he had received from the instrument panel.

"Hmm." Gregor locked both hands around his head. An idea was beginning to form in the back of his mind. It was pretty tenuous, but under the circumstances . . .

"I am now scanning the island," the lifeboat announced.

Looking out the forward porthole, Gregor and Arnold could see the island, no more than a hundred yards away. The first flush of dawn was in the sky, and outlined against it was the scarred, beloved snout of their spaceship.

"Place looks fine to me," Arnold said.

"It sure does," Gregor agreed. "I'll bet our forces are dug in underground."

"They are not," the lifeboat said. "I scanned to a depth of a hundred feet."

"Well," Arnold said, "under the circumstances, I think we should examine a little more closely. I'd better go ashore and look around."

"It is deserted," the lifeboat said. "Believe me, my senses are infinitely more acute than yours. I cannot let you endanger your lives by going ashore. Drome needs her soldiers —especially sturdy, heat-resistant types like you."

"We like this climate," Arnold said.

"Spoken like a patriot!" the lifeboat said heartily. "I know how you must be suffering. But now I am going to the south pole, to give you veterans the rest you deserve."

Gregor decided it was time for his plan, no matter how vague it was. "That won't be necessary," he said.

"What?"

"We are operating under special orders," Gregor said. "We weren't supposed to disclose them to any vessel below the rank of super-dreadnaught. But under the circumstances—"

"Yes, under the circumstances," Arnold chimed in eagerly, "we will tell you."

"We are a suicide squad," Gregor said.

"Especially trained for hot climate work."

"Our orders," Gregor said, "are to land and secure that island for the Drome forces."

"I didn't know that," the boat said.

"You weren't supposed to," Arnold told it. "After all, you're only a lifeboat."

"Land us at once," Gregor said. "There's no time to lose."

"You should have told me sooner," the boat said. "I couldn't guess, you know." It began to move toward the island

Gregor could hardly breathe. It didn't seem possible that the simple trick would work. But then, why not? The lifeboat was built to accept the word of its operators as the truth. As long as the 'truth' was consistent with the boat's operational premises, it would be carried out.

The beach was only fifty yards away now, gleaming white in the cold light of dawn.

Then the boat reversed its engines and stopped. "No," it said.

"No what?"

"I cannot do it."

"What do you mean?" Arnold shouted. "This is war! Orders—"

"I know," the lifeboat said sadly. "I am sorry. A different type of vessel should have been chosen for this mission. Any other type. But not a *lifeboat*."

"You must," Gregor begged. "Think of our country, think of the barbaric H'gen—"

"It is physically impossible for me to carry out your orders," the lifeboat told them. "My prime directive is to protect my occupants from harm. That order is stamped on my every tape, giving priority over all others. I cannot let you go to your certain death."

The boat began to move away from the island.

"You'll be court-martialed for this!" Arnold screamed hysterically. "They'll decommission you."

"I must operate within my limitations," the boat said sadly. "If we find the fleet, I will transfer you to a killerboat. But in the meantime, I must take you to the safety of the south pole."

The lifeboat picked up speed, and the island receded behind them. Arnold rushed at the controls and was thrown flat. Gregor picked up the canteen and poised it, to hurl ineffectually at the sealed hatch. He stopped himself in mid-swing, struck by a sudden wild thought.

"Please don't attempt any more destruction," the boat pleaded. "I know how you feel, but—"

It was damned risky, Gregor thought, but the south pole was certain death anyhow.

He uncapped the canteen. "Since we cannot accomplish our mission," he said, "we can never again face our comrades. Suicide is the only alternative." He took a gulp of water and handed the canteen to Arnold.

"No! Don't!" the lifeboat shrieked. "That's *water!* It's a deadly poison—"

An electrical bolt leaped from the instrument panel, knocking the canteen from Arnold's hand.

Arnold grabbed the canteen. Before the boat could knock it again from his hand, he had taken a drink.

"We die for glorious Drome!" Gregor dropped to the floor. He motioned Arnold to lie still.

"There is no known antidote," the boat moaned. "If only I could contact a hospital ship . . ." Its engines idled indecisively. "Speak to me," the boat pleaded. "Are you still alive?"

Gregor and Arnold lay perfectly still, not breathing.

"Answer me!" the lifeboat begged. "Perhaps if you ate some geezel . . ." It thrust out two trays. The partners didn't stir.

"Dead," the lifeboat said. "Dead. I will read the burial service."

There was a pause. Then the lifeboat intoned, "Great Spirit of the Universe, take into your custody the souls of these, your servants. Although they died by their own hand, still it was in the service of their country, fighting for home and hearth. Judge them not harshly for their impious deed. Rather blame the spirit of war that inflames and destroys all Drome."

The hatch swung open. Gregor could feel a rush of cool morning air.

"And now, by the authority vested in me by the Drome Fleet, and with all reverence, I commer 1 their bodies to the deep."

Gregor felt himself being lifted through the hatch to the deck. Then he was in the air, falling, and in another moment he was in the water, with Arnold beside him.

"Float quietly," he whispered.

The island was nearby. But the lifeboat was still hovering close to them, nervously roaring its engines.

"What do you think it's up to now?" Arnold whispered.

"I don't know," Gregor said, hoping that the Drome peoples didn't believe in converting their bodies to ashes.

The lifeboat came closer. Its bow was only a few feet away. They tensed. And then they heard it. The roaring screech of the Drome National Anthem.

In a moment it was finished. The lifeboat murmured, "Rest in peace," turned, and roared away.

As they swam slowly to the island, Gregor saw that the lifeboat was heading south, due south, to the pole, to wait for the Drome fleet.